Also by Steven Barwin
in the Lorimer Sports Stories series

Fadeaway
Icebreaker
Making Select
SK8ER
Rock Dogs

SPIKED
Steven Barwin

James Lorimer & Company Ltd., Publishers
Toronto

James Lorimer & Company Ltd., Publishers acknowledges the support of the Ontario Arts Council. We acknowledge the financial support of the Government of Canada through the Canada Book Fund for our publishing activities. We acknowledge the support of the Canada Council for the Arts which last year invested $24.3 million in writing and publishing throughout Canada. We acknowledge the Government of Ontario through the Ontario Media Development Corporation's Ontario Book Initiative.

Cover image: iStock

Library and Archives Canada Cataloguing in Publication

Barwin, Steven, author
        Spiked / Steven Barwin.

(Sports stories)
Issued in print and electronic formats.
ISBN 978-1-4594-0527-1 (bound).--ISBN 978-1-4594-0528-8 (pbk.).--
ISBN 978-1-4594-0529-5 (epub)

        I. Title. II. Series: Sports stories (Toronto, Ont.)

PS8553.A7836S65 2013   jC813'.54   C2013-904187-7   C2013-904188-5

James Lorimer & Company Ltd.,
Publishers
317 Adelaide Street West, Suite 1002
Toronto, ON, Canada
M5V 1P9
www.lorimer.ca

Distributed in the United States by:
Orca Book Publishers
P.O. Box 468
Custer, WA, USA
98240-0468

Printed and bound in Canada.
Manufactured by Friesens Corporation in Altona, Manitoba, Canada in August 2013.
Job # 87606

To my children, nieces and nephews, don't let your friends determine what you do. Make good choices that are right for you.

CONTENTS

1 SINGING THE BLUES

"Worst day of school ever," I grumbled.

Hailey pressed out a small crease on her skinny jeans and nodded. She flicked back her jet-black hair, looking like the perfect ten I'll never be. "Emma, there are more important things in life than marks, you know."

Claire agreed, "She's right. Actually, you're right too. That math test was a killer."

I grabbed my binder and did a quick makeup check in the mirror on my locker door. Claire squeezed in front of me, pushing her sandy brown hair behind her ears. When she stepped back, I shut my locker and followed them to class. "Come on, Claire," I said. "Your marks are always great. You're on easy street."

She smiled because she knew I was right.

"It's not the marks; it's dealing with parents — but that's easy. Just create a bigger fire," Hailey offered, "and then bad marks won't seem so bad."

"What kind of fire?" I asked.

"Something small. Throw a party, get a tattoo, get

9

caught stealing money from them. Just pick one."

I laughed out loud. "Sounds like you've done them all."

"Those are just my fires. You should see my explosions."

Claire looked at me, her eyes a little wider. "A tattoo, eh? A unicorn above your ankle would look great."

"All great ideas, Hailey," I said. "You know, you should've run for student president."

Hailey frowned. "Yes, things need to change in this school. But have you seen how grotesque student council is? Have they heard of personal hygiene? Like, 'It's called a shower. Use it.'"

I laughed again, and then stopped as a grade eight boy blocked me. "How you doing today, Emma?"

I looked down at him. "What's up, Connor?"

"Not much." He had big hair and a goofball smile, and he wouldn't meet my eyes.

"Okay, well, have a good day, Connor."

"There was something I wanted to ask you."

Hailey stepped in. "Enjoying the view?"

He smirked at her. "What are you talking about?"

I realized that his eyes were even with my chest. I quickly crossed my arms in front of myself.

Hailey pushed him aside, and I quickly walked away.

"You okay?" Claire asked, following me.

I nodded and fought back a tear. "I'm a freak of nature."

Hailey caught up without seeming to hurry. "I can't believe you keep falling for that, Emma. But you're missing the *bigger* picture." She laughed at her own joke. I didn't see what there was to laugh about. "Remember when that supply teacher asked you for directions to the teacher's lounge?"

"Yeah? So?"

"Just saying, you're taller than half the teachers."

"God, thanks for making me feel better, Hailey."

"You don't get what I'm saying," Hailey said. "Emma, your being a giant is a gift. You can pass for a Grade Twelve."

"And?"

"High-school boys have cars."

"She has a point," Claire said.

Hailey might have what it takes to date high-school guys, but I couldn't even get up the nerve to talk to Jeremy. It didn't help that I towered over him.

Hailey said, "Just smile and remember who saved you from being a nobody."

Claire jumped in. "That's not nice!"

"Same goes for you, too, Claire," Hailey said.

I thought back to how everything had been fine — I was into sports and being a little taller was a good thing. And then in grade five I shot up and became a freak. My mind flooded with memories of being called *upper deck* and *top shelf*, and being asked, "How's the weather up there?" Then I remembered how good it felt when super-cool and beautiful Hailey showed up, telling me that my height made me supermodel material.

"So don't let the people beneath you get under your perfect skin. Okay?" Hailey laughed again. "*Beneath you*. Get it?"

I followed my friends into Mr. Marshall's math class. Surviving it was impossible without Hailey and Claire. At my seat, I felt a small, muffled vibration and smiled. Like all our teachers, Mr. Marshall had moved us to opposite corners of the classroom, but he could never truly separate us.

Hailey: bored already

I didn't need to wait for Mr. Marshall to turn to the board before replying. My hand was on my phone in my right pocket, and from where the teacher was standing it looked like I was just resting my hand on my lap. My phone vibrated again and I snuck a peek at the text.

Claire: yes back on the teach

I pushed the home button, swiped to unlock and was in the messages app. Back at the home button, my thumb moved up four spaces to the letter *t*. From there I was on autopilot. I had the location of all the numbers and letters memorized. If I made a mistake, autocorrect would take care of it.

Emma: oh right.

I nodded at Mr. Marshall as if I were deep in thought and his words were seeping into my brain like it was a sponge.

Emma: so bored.

I gave Mr. Marshall a look like I was getting smarter by the second. *Multiplying the numerator by the denominator is so much more fun than adding the numerator by the denominator. Thank you, Mr. Marshall, for I have seen the light!*

Emma: shoot me.

Claire: What's three times four?

I snickered out loud and Mr. Marshall's eyes targeted me. "Problem?"

"No."

"How about an apology for interrupting the class?" He took a sip of coffee while waiting for me to reply. Just another sip of thousands, riding his coffee wave all the way to summer vacation while watching my every move. A month ago I wondered how much money Tim Horton's made off Mr. Marshall, so I tracked his intake at two cups a day. I assumed he has plain coffee and not the fancy stuff, and just included schooldays. It comes to more than eighteen bucks a week, or $720 a year, plus tax. *See Mr. Marshall,* I thought, *I can do math.*

"What's it going to be?"

"Sorry, everyone."

"Now, back to work."

People around me looked up. I just wanted to get back to my phone.

Hailey: lol.

Claire: So sorry!!!

Hailey: 6 months 2 go.

She was right. Six months and we were off to high school. I squirmed in my seat as the minutes dragged on like hours. Two washroom breaks later, the first-term report cards appeared in Mr. Marshall's hands. "Okay, class, bell's about to go."

Emma: i feel sick.

Hailey: nobody ever fails.

Mr. Marshall suddenly appeared in front of me. "You know the rule. No cell phones in the classroom."

I stared back at him.

"Who are you texting with?"

I said nothing, but my eyes darted to Hailey for a split second.

"Hailey, over here. Now."

Hailey threw me an ugly look as she walked to my desk.

"Is Emma texting you?" Mr. Marshall asked.

Hailey shrugged her shoulders. "No."

"You sure about that?"

"Yeah, it's not me this time. But Emma's always texting in class."

"Isn't that interesting." Mr. Marshall held out his hand to me. "Give me the phone."

I placed it in his hand.

"I don't even have a phone on me." Hailey held her arms out. "Go ahead, frisk me, officer."

Mr. Marshall didn't bite. "Emma, if you want to see this again, your parents can come and pick it up. I need to see them anyway to talk about this." He dropped my report card on my desk. I took the innocent-looking brown envelope, knowing that inside was a bomb waiting to go off.

2 PITCH BLACK

Kaboom.

Except for the scraping of forks and knives on their plates, my parents were dead quiet at dinner. It was weird how me throwing away my future could suck the air out of the dining room. This was definitely the bad kind of quiet.

I was back in my room and on my computer with the door closed when I detected the first grumbling. At first I thought it might have been the heater. I turned on my music.

I turned back to my screen to Hailey and Claire in a Facebook chat box. Claire, an adorable goofball, had Mr. Krabs from SpongeBob as her profile picture. Hailey's was a stunning glossy head shot, like the ones supermodels have in their portfolios. I remember having to take it over and over again until it was perfect. Every year since grade six I'd been updating it for her.

The grumbling increased below me. It became clear that Mom and Dad were starting to argue, and it was about me. The voices below grew louder. I cranked the music.

Hailey and Claire were typing mean but true things about people at school. I wasn't in the mood to bad-mouth others when I wasn't feeling too hot about *moi*. I went to my bookmarks and opened my favourite blog. It seemed that *Tall Girl Tells All* was written just for me. Finding clothes impossible? Me too. Going XL meant the sleeves were the right length, but I looked like I was drowning in a parachute. Buying clothes because they looked good only meant returning them and then going to a big-and-tall store. I knew those places all too well. That's where embarrassment and social catastrophe lived.

I picked up the landline for the first time in years and hit the autodial for Claire.

She was surprised to find me on the phone. "I thought your mom was calling me!"

"Sucks that I have to use this. I feel like a part of me is missing without my cell phone. I can't talk long because I don't want my parents to catch me."

"How's everything there?"

"Let's just say that today's not been a great day."

"Tomorrow will be better."

"How? I'll still be an oversized creature in Barbie-doll world."

"And what does that make me? A troll?"

"No! Claire, you're perfect."

"Just give me some of your height to balance out my weight. About a metre should do it."

"Don't be a dope, Claire." I knew where Claire's image of herself as fat came from. "How's Hailey?"

"Oh, right. You almost got her in trouble, but it's okay now."

"So it's okay that I get in trouble as long as Hailey doesn't?"

"What?" Claire asked.

"Because of her, I got into so much hot water."

"That's Hailey for you."

The sounds of fighting downstairs spiked through the music, and I told Claire I had to go. A part of me wished that they would just come in and yell at me. Let me have it, tell me how I only care about being popular and then ground me or whatever.

★★★

My mother worked her magic and managed to get an appointment at the school first thing the next morning. Sitting in front of Mr. Marshall and his coffee in the school's conference room downstairs, he started to blab about my academics. "So let's talk report card first, Ms. Jackson. Based on what I'm seeing in class, this report card comes as no surprise. Emma's a very smart girl who doesn't try at all. But what I'm really worried about is high school."

My mom, totally on his side, was nodding like a bobblehead.

"I'd like to hear from Emma," he continued. "Are you concerned?"

I shrugged. My mom nudged me, but I didn't say anything.

"Here's the issue. If you want to go to university you need to take the academic stream. I'm not sure what kind of career you might want, but I think you're going to have a hard time surviving academic the way you're going."

"Are you listening?" my mom asked with an edge to her voice.

"One term is gone and that leaves only two for you to improve. We want the best for you, and second term starts today. But you have to want to make the change."

Suffering through the get-together, I would've given anything to have Claire's parents. All they ask from her is that she tries her best.

"Part of solving this issue is to rethink the kind of friends you're hanging out with." Mr. Marshall placed my cell phone on the table. "You were texting with Hailey in class yesterday, weren't you?"

I shook my head.

"I've always threatened to take that thing away," my mom said. "But it's the only way I can keep in contact with her when she's out with her friends."

Mr. Marshall gave her the phone.

My mother looked at it and said, "I'm sorry Emma has wasted her time and yours. You've got twenty-nine other students whose time she has wasted, too. Emma owes more than an apology. There needs to be a punishment."

Mr. Marshall nodded.

"Maybe she can help in class. Owing you time would be a good way of repaying you for her wasting your time."

"I could always use the help. I coach the girls volleyball team."

Help me now! I screamed in my head.

"Emma," my mom said, "you played volleyball a few years ago."

"I remember," Mr. Marshall smiled. "I was her coach."

I crossed my arms. "I'm not playing volleyball."

"You can volunteer on the team," offered Mr. Marshall. "I always need help during practices and games."

"Wonderful idea," my mom said, pleased as can be.

"No, Mom. I can't do that."

"Why not?"

What would Hailey think? The end of my social life was playing out in my head. First Hailey would disown me. Then she'd publicly humiliate me until I was nothing.

My mom kept her gaze on me. "You don't do anything anymore except hang out with your friends. Even when you're home, you're with them on your phone, on the computer . . ."

Mr. Marshall nodded.

I grabbed my mom's hand. "No, Mom, please."

"Well, Emma, something has to change. You can't keep getting away with not trying in school." My mom looked at me and then smiled at Mr. Marshall. "Looks like you've got a helper." The first bell rang and ended the interrogation. I dragged my backpack upstairs.

I heard a voice behind me. "Your mom's really nice. She only wants the best for you."

I turned to see Mr. Marshall. "I'm late for class."

"Me, too. We both have math."

With each step, I slammed my foot down. At the top of the stairs, my anger was at an all-time high. I made sure it was just the two of us in the stairwell, and then turned to confront Mr. Marshall. "I don't appreciate being volun-*told* what to do with my life."

He nodded. "Adults call it slave labour. But it's good for you. Plus, you'll be grateful for the head start on collecting those volunteer hours when you get to high school."

I wasn't going to take advice from a man who wears a whistle.

At the top of the stairs, he caught up with me and held the door open. "You'll find it's an easy gig."

"Is this your way of getting me to play on your team?"

"I'm not recruiting you. The team's already been picked."

I walked past him and got into line for class next to Hailey.

"What was that about?" she asked.

"Nothing." Little did I know that my whole life was about to disappear into a black hole.

3 WHITE NOISE

The doors opened and Mr. Marshall waved me over to the middle of the gym. I had to go around the court where girls were hitting the ball back and forth. I remembered playing volleyball. I remembered having to ice my sore wrists.

"You're late," he said accusingly.

"I'm here."

"Flip the brass floor plates, and I'll show you how to put up the net."

"Huh?"

He pointed to two brown covers on the floor. I lifted them, revealing a hole in the gym floor.

"Now you take the uprights and put them in. When they stop turning, they're in."

I lifted a red bar into the hole. As I turned it, the volleyball net stretched out until it was tight. I checked out the team. They were all nobodies.

"That's it?" I asked.

"Yes."

"Okay. See ya."

"Hold on. The deal was that you're here for practice. See that water bottle?"

I nodded.

"Fill it."

Rolling my eyes, I grabbed it and headed for the drinking fountain. I checked my phone in the hallway. I had twenty texts and e-mails asking where I was. I had to make up an excuse for being out of touch.

Emma: phone's losing it. need a charge.

When I came back, the team was on one side of the net and Mr. Marshall stood on the other.

He called out to the players, "When you're returning your serve, keep your hands in the ready position so you can pass high or low. You want your knees bent so, if it comes low, you can make a slight move forward with the hips and let the ball rebound off your landing pad." He might as well have been speaking another language.

He dug volleyballs out of a wire cart, and the girls lined up to return his serve. Some got the ball on target, but most barely made it over the net.

I held out the water bottle in front of Mr. Marshall's face.

All eyes turned to me.

"I almost forgot," Mr. Marshall announced. "This is our new team assistant, Emma."

The girls all looked at me as if I were a science

project or a zoo animal. I tried to ignore their eyes as I shook the water bottle.

Mr. Marshall grabbed it and took a sip. "Not bad. I prefer it colder, so next time let the water run."

The girls laughed. At least they weren't looking at me anymore. Mr. Marshall told the team to divide up and practice. He led me to the side of the court. "I remember when you were in grade four," he said quietly. "You were an excellent athlete."

All I remember was being bullied for being a jock. What was I thinking, coming back to all this?

"I understand that this isn't ideal, so I have another offer for you," said Mr. Marshall when I didn't reply. "Trade in the helper job for playing on the team. You might as well have fun, plus you will still make up the time you owe me."

Suddenly I saw the light. "You tricked me!" I said. "This was a set-up."

"Not at all."

"Why do you want me to play? Because I'm taller than anyone on your team?"

"Hey, having you help me was your mom's call. I'm just trying to see if everyone can benefit from it."

A girl from the team walked over. "Coach? You want us doing this drill all practice?"

Mr. Marshall said, "Emma, this is Zoe. She's our team captain."

Like that meant anything to me. The girl and I

exchanged the quickest of glances.

"Emma was just going to clean out the locker room," Mr. Marshall said with a sigh.

I stomped across the court, right through the drill. The locker room was disgusting. And the worst part was that I couldn't get a signal.

★★★

At lunch the next day, Hailey used her phone's camera to check her hair. "So you have to spend all this time in a sweaty gym?"

"This was my mom's cruel idea."

Claire said, "I feel for you. So, do you, like, have to . . . What do you do?"

Hailey jumped in. "Clean sweat off the floor?"

The girls *eww*ed together.

Claire grabbed Hailey's phone to check her hair. "Too bad it isn't the boys' team."

"Claire," said Hailey, noticing Claire's sandwich "You're not going to eat that, are you?"

"Oh, um," Claire mumbled. I could tell she suddenly lost her appetite. Hailey was always going on about how everything Claire ate went straight to her "big butt." Claire got up to throw away her lunch, and I was going to say something to Hailey when she turned on me.

"Well," Hailey started, "I don't know if I can still be friends with you."

"For real? Why?" I asked.

Claire took a photo of my dismayed look with Hailey's phone before I could cover my face.

Hailey grabbed the phone and looked at it. "Little more mascara, little more leg — and ask Mr. Marshall to fire you."

Hailey held the picture out to show me, and I screeched.

"Delete it. Now!"

Claire laughed. "Emma, you're beautiful."

I grabbed for the phone. "Nah-ah."

"I know what we should do," Hailey said. "Let's post your pic and let the netizens be the judge. That way you'll know for sure."

"No," I responded quickly. "Remember when those grade eight girls did that last year?"

"Emma's right," Claire nodded. "Those girls got into so much trouble."

"That's because they were stupid enough to post their names," Hailey snorted. "We'll just do your picture."

"People still might recognize me." I was getting worried that Hailey wasn't just kidding around.

"Who? Random Internet strangers?"

"What do you think?" I asked Claire.

"I wouldn't want my face online," she said firmly.

"I agree."

"And if we all do it?" Hailey asked.

"Answer's still no," I said.

"Okay," Hailey sighed. "You guys are no fun."

Over her shoulder I spotted some of the volleyball girls coming into the lunchroom. I turned away, but it was too late.

"Hey, Emma," Zoe said.

I looked at her, then at Hailey. How was this going to play out?

I didn't say anything. Hailey would kill me for talking to a jock, an average-looking girl who wore a headband to hold back hair that was in serious need of some styling.

"This is Victoria," Zoe went on, as if we were actually having a conversation.

Her friend was her bad-hair-day clone. It was clear they weren't going away until I said something. The moment I said hi to Victoria, Hailey and Claire turned their backs.

Zoe waved as they walked away. "See you around."

Hailey, her back still to me, asked, "Gone?"

"Yep," I answered.

She turned. "Thank god. Those girls are disgusting. You need to quit before you start smelling like them."

"She's right," Claire added. "Those ugly ducklings can't be seen talking to us swans."

Hailey went for a high-five. "Nice one."

Claire took a bow, "Thank you."

They turned to me, palms held up. I high-fived

Claire, but Hailey quickly dropped her hand. "She didn't get her stink on you, did she?"

4 RUST

Players entered the hot, loud gym. I seriously considered making a run for it. *Too bad mom knows when they play,* I thought. The team's green and yellow jerseys showed a Viking helmet. I sat on a bench as far away as possible from two girls who were clearly not good enough to be included in the game.

Mr. Marshall stood up, his golf shirt half-untucked. "First game of the season, Vikings! Always bump and set the play."

My eyes found my phone at my side. I had bigger problems than a volleyball game, like getting a signal. I was down to one bar.

Emma: watcha guys doing?

Claire: At the mall

Emma: wish i was there

Claire: Me 2. Hailey is making me buy a shirt

Emma: u at gap?

A shadow appeared over my screen. I looked up at Mr. Marshall. "Give me the phone," he said, frowning.

I tucked it in my pocket.

"Your time is my time. Don't let me see it again." He pointed to a row of water bottles at the bench. "See those? Fill them."

"All of them?"

His answer was drowned out by the loud cheering signalling that the game had started. The other team smashed the ball into our court. I smiled when Zoe dove for it and missed.

Mr. Marshall clapped his hands loudly, "Come on, girls. Pick it up and move on!"

I used the distraction and sat back down on the bench, phone already out.

Emma: sorry bout that

Mr. Marshall coughed loudly in my direction. I shoved the phone back in my pocket and took off with the water bottles.

I was relieved to find the hallway empty. I sighed repeatedly as the fountain slowly leaked into the first of eight bottles.

At least filling the bottles got me out of the gym. When I got back to the bench, I rattled the bottles as loudly as I could.

Mr. Marshall must have called a timeout. All the players were gathered around him. "At the net, they're hitting the ball cross-court . . ."

I let the bottles clang to the bench.

He paused and said without even looking at me,

"Hand them out to the players."

"But, how do —"

"Use the numbers."

There was a jersey number on each of the bottles. *What is this, kindergarten?* I thought.

"Where was I?" Mr. Marshall said. "They're hitting cross-court and finding our corners."

I called out, "Number seven?"

He glanced at me, frustrated. "Everyone get your own water."

The girls rushed at me as Mr. Marshall called me over with his finger. I dropped the bottles.

"Don't like this, Emma?"

"No. Not really. Surprised, Mr. Marshall?"

"Out here, *Coach* will do just fine."

"Mr. Coach?"

"You know you can join the team."

That again. I turned back to the bench. "No thanks."

"Okay. Pick up that that pile of face towels and put them on the bench."

The other team's coach called out to us. "Hey, Marshall, if you're not going to use errand girl, we'll take her." He chuckled and turned away.

Coach Marshall tapped my shoulder. "You see, I'm not the only person to see your potential."

"Whatever."

Before I could sit down, he said, "Face towels. And they have numbers on them too."

"I could quit right now, you know."

"You're your own person. You can do whatever you want." He grabbed a jersey and shorts from behind the bench. "Or you could put this on and join the Spikin' Vikings."

"Rather quit."

I looked at the towels and thought of the awful locker room.

"One more thing, Emma," his voice broke into my misery. "My Viking mascot got a part-time job." He pointed to a kid running around in a one-piece Viking suit, wearing a long yellow beard and a helmet with horns. "You can wear the mascot suit or the jersey. Your choice."

"No!" I was horrified. This was a nightmare, and it didn't look like I would be waking up anytime soon.

Coach Marshall smiled. "Then I'm subbing you in."

It was blackmail, but I couldn't see any way out of it. I went to the locker room and took a long time to put on the jersey. I came out, my hands over my face. "I can't play in my boots."

Coach Marshall held up a pair of sneakers. "You can borrow these." Could this get any grosser?

"Take the middle blocker position," he said.

"I don't remember the game."

"It's only been two years. Don't worry about it, we're losing horribly. You can't make it much worse."

"But —"

"Just stand at the net with your arms straight up."

On the court, someone was kind enough to point me in the right direction — front row and centre. Hands up, I used my arms to deflect stares from both teams.

The other team served the ball, and the Vikings sprang into action. Victoria deflected the ball to a girl who passed it to the girl next to me. She slammed it over the net. The other team managed to get to it and sent the ball soaring in the air — right toward me.

Coach Marshall threw his hands in the air.

I pushed my arms up, copying him. I barely had time to notice that I could raise them as high as the top of the net.

The ball hammered off my hands. It dropped like a stone, just making it over the net. It hit the ground.

The coach bounced up and down. The player next to me gave me a quick pat on the back. What had I done?

Zoe leaned in. "Good job. You won us the serve."

5 GREENHORN

I was last in and out of the locker room. Coach Marshall gave me an unpleasant look.

"Late for practice again."

I looked at my uniform and kneepads and gasped. *What am I doing?* I thought. *I look like them.*

Making my entrance into the gym, I noticed that nobody stared at me this time. Coach Marshall fished a volleyball out of a blue holder on legs. "We're practicing serves. One foot in front. With your left hand, balance the ball. Then bring the ball up straight. You're going to hit it with your right hand."

He bounced the ball at me. I grabbed it and held it in my left hand, my feet in position.

"Step and make contact with one hand."

I smacked the ball at him.

"Don't let your hand cross over. Stop it like you're about to wave at the person across from you."

Great, sweating already.

"Got it?"

"Yep."

"Join in over here." Coach Marshall led me to where Zoe was practicing her serve with a partner.

Zoe stepped out so I could serve to her partner. I would've been happy sitting it out until someone was open. Instead, the ball I served got caught in the net.

Zoe shifted to captain mode right away. "Come on girls," she clapped. "*Spikin' Vikings, you can do it!*"

That annoying rant — sorry, *chant* — was going to stick in my head all day. A few more back and forths and my sweat level was beyond anything Hailey would ever tolerate. The year before, Hailey had tried to talk the gym teacher into letting her, Claire, and me sit with the religious girls. They had notes to get them out of gym. When that didn't work, we joined in only up until the point of first sweat. Then it was washroom breaks and fake asthma attacks. I could hear her voice in my head: *It's called a shower. Use it!*

Coach blew his whistle. Like little robots, everyone else stopped and sat on the ground around him. I took my time.

"It all starts here," he said. "The serve is a critical part of our game. It's less about power and more about accuracy. If you can get the ball in play deep in their zone, it makes the return volley harder for them and gives us the advantage. Let's try it again."

I was back on the line next to Zoe, who was so excited she was chirpy. She ran through the list of players' names for me, which I guess was nice. I remembered Victoria, but the only way I'd know the whole team was if first names were on their uniforms.

I waited for Coach Marshall to help my partner with her serve. "So, no offence, but has the team always sucked?" I asked Zoe.

"We don't suck. Far from it."

"But that other team destroyed you last game."

"That was the Warriors. They're the best team in the league. They win every school tourney." Zoe pointed at banners hanging up high on the wall. "And we get second every time."

I looked at the banners until my neck hurt, but that wasn't very long. "And the coach thinks that bringing in someone tall is going to change all that?"

"Couldn't hurt."

I threw her a look that said her comment was not cool.

"What?" she said. "Is it so wrong to want to win?"

"Guess not."

Zoe set herself up for a serve, pausing to say, "And you are tall. It's a good thing. I wish I was as tall as you."

Never heard that before, I thought.

"Okay!" Coach Marshall called out, "Now let's get in a line and go one-on-one."

Zoe signalled for me to step behind her. "After I serve, they'll serve back and you grab the ball and stand where I am," she explained just before she smashed the ball over the net.

"That's how it's done," Coach Marshall called over. He clapped.

Then the ball came to me. Every eye was on me as I took position to serve. My skills were rusty and everybody could tell.

Coach Marshall stepped in, moving me into the correct position like a mannequin. "Serving hand up. Elbow above your shoulder. Hold the ball horizontal to your shoulders. Toss it."

I fumbled the serve. If I didn't want to play volleyball, why did it feel so bad that I sucked at it?

"Nice try," said Coach Marshall. He took the ball and stood in front of me with his hand up high. "High-five me." I don't know what I had done to rate a high-five, but I did what he said.

"Harder. Really slap my hand."

I did.

"Now with the ball."

My right hand extended to the back of the ball, slapping it. The ball arced over the net. It was like my body still remembered how much push to give it. "Good, right?"

"Yeah." But he went on to say, "Except for the foot fault. And lift. You have to step into it and drag your back foot forward. And don't drop the elbow. But you did great."

Gee, thanks. "Okay," Coach Marshall called out, "good practice. Make sure you all have rides to the game at Pendray Junior High."

Zoe rushed up to offer me a lift. When I didn't jump at the offer, she insisted that I join her.

As the pack of girls headed to the locker room, I heard Coach Marshall call my name. "What, Coach?"

"The team may not say it, but you're good. The other game, you helped save us from an embarrassing loss."

"Are you saying I'm a natural? Best talent you've ever seen in all your years . . ."

He smiled. "Don't be afraid to use your height advantage. It's a good thing."

Just before I disappeared into the locker room, I got in the last word. "Don't get used to me. As soon as I convince my mom, I'm outta here."

6 GREEN WITH ENVY

My baggy shorts, running shoes, and tank top were replaced by skinny jeans, comfy Ugg boots, and an Abercrombie & Fitch hoodie — and it couldn't be soon enough. I dodged the old people who were scattered around the mall like litter and found the girls. While they grabbed deals like pirates looting a treasure ship, I stayed clear of the XL rack. A pair of earrings that my mom would definitely make me return caught my eye.

"Gotta be honest, Em," Hailey said between sips of bubble tea as we left the store. "Being a gym helper is wreaking havoc on your skin."

Claire laughed, her mouth around the straw stuck in her diet pop. "Breakout warning!"

"It's because of other people's sweat," Hailey laughed loudly.

I nodded, knowing that it was also my own sweat. What would Hailey think about me being on the team? I scanned my face and found a small red dot shining like a beacon.

"Hey, guys," Hailey interrupted my secret thoughts. "look who it is."

Jeremy approached with three other guys. "What's up, girls?" he said casually.

Hailey lifted her shopping bag. "Not much." Hailey's bag was obviously heavier than Claire's or mine. She had dropped a hundred on her emergency credit card, and she wasn't done yet.

I couldn't decide what I liked more — Jeremy's straight, almost-black hair or his green eyes. Except for being short — well, shorter than me — he was perfect.

In an attempt to reduce my height disadvantage on Jeremy, I bent my knees without trying to look like an idiot. "Yeah, shopping." Right away my back started to hurt. I moved away from Claire who made me look even taller.

"That's cool. My boys and I are just wandering around."

"This mall could use a few more stores." Hailey smiled up into Jeremy's eyes.

"You're so right. This place needs an Apple store."

"That's exactly what I was thinking," I said.

He held up his hand for a high-five and we joined hands. It might've just been for a moment, but I sensed something. I think he did too.

Jeremy said, "We thought about going to a movie, but there's nothing good on."

We all stopped talking when a mall security guy walked past and gave us a suspicious look.

"What's with that?" I asked.

Jeremy said, "Pay sucks, job sucks, his life sucks. So he takes it out on us."

I laughed.

"Anyway," he continued, "I think we're just going to go to the skating rink and laugh at people when they wipe out. Want to come?"

I nodded. "Sounds great —"

"Actually," Hailey interrupted, "we have more shopping to do. Maybe we'll meet up with you after."

Jeremy said, "Okay." And he was gone.

I turned to Hailey. "I wanted to go. He's never asked me to do anything."

"Us. He asked *us*," she said. "Don't sound so desperate. Trust me on this one. If you say yes right away, then you're like a loser with nothing better to do than wait around for him. This way he'll think you've got your own thing going on, and he'll be extra happy to see you." She took off to the next store.

"Why do we put up with her, Claire?" I asked.

"Because she's beautiful, charming, and popular?"

"Good point."

"Emma, we better catch up with her. You know how she doesn't like to shop alone."

I nodded and followed Claire following Hailey.

Hailey had stopped in front of a sports store to wait

for us. She looked at me impatiently.

"Want to go in there?" I asked Hailey.

"No, but you probably do."

Claire laughed. I thought about telling Hailey that Claire had been on the grade-five chess team. Hailey would flip. At least it would take her attention off me.

Hailey snickered and moved past the sports store. "Oh, look. It's Mr. Marshall!"

"No way!" I covered my face. Then I spread my fingers to peer between them. There was no one there.

Hailey could barely contain herself, laughing so hard she almost dropped her bags. "You totally freaked out!"

"It's because I didn't want him to see me, Hailey."

"Are you into older guys?" Claire asked.

The two of them howled loudly, upsetting a group of elderly men who were hogging the mall chairs.

Claire added, "It's cool. Relax. Just a bad joke."

So maybe Claire had *some* sympathy for her so-called best friend in the universe.

Hailey propped herself up to put her arm around my shoulders. "Isn't Claire the funniest person you know?"

I smiled. I figured the least I could do was to be a good sport. If I couldn't take what I'm usually dishing, why would I be friends with Hailey?

Hailey clearly thought I had been the centre of attention for too long. She started to blab about herself on our way to one of her favourite clothes stores.

With one foot barely in the door, I saw Zoe and

Victoria inside. *Is everyone at this stupid mall today?!* I wondered. "Guys," I said to Claire and Hailey, "let's go back. I need to get a new cover for my phone."

Claire took my hand and dragged me into the store. "You buy a new cover every week."

I sighed and thought about throwing a tantrum. Instead, I walked straight to the front corner and took cover by a wheeled rack of clothes to be put on display. This broke Hailey's girl's guide to shopping. "Start near the checkout and do a figure eight," she'd say. "And that's how you shop smart." The only thing I cared about was turning invisible. Easier said than done.

"Today's our Wacky Wednesday sale."

"Can I help you?" a saleslady asked me in a piercing voice. "Today's our Wacky Wednesday sale."

I wanted to shush her. I wanted to tell her that if business was that bad they should close shop before coming up with something so lame. Or have products for people who aren't short and thin and perfect. I shooed her away.

"Well, let me know if you need help," she said in a peeved voice.

Turning back to the corner, I yelped like a poodle as Hailey and Claire appeared in front of me.

Hailey beckoned with her finger. "Come on, Em, we found something that's gonna fit you perfectly."

"One minute." I scurried in the opposite direction, poking my head up among the taller racks. There was no sign of anyone until — *wham!* — Zoe and Victoria appeared like a bad mirage.

Zoe offered an, "Oh, hi."

"Hi," I mumbled.

"Shopping by yourself?" Victoria asked.

I nodded, but then my stupid lie was crushed when Hailey and Claire found us.

"So," Zoe started, but the look on Hailey's face squashed any hope for normal conversation.

Victoria bravely tried. "Your friend Emma's a big help to our volleyball team."

Hailey, arms crossed, asked, "What are you talking about?"

"The Spikin' Vikings," Victoria explained.

"English, please."

I couldn't take it anymore, so I jumped in. "Remember, my mom and Mr. Marshall forced me because of the texting in class —"

Zoe nodded. "So that's the story. Good to know."

Hailey and Claire looked like they were enjoying the encounter. "So," Hailey said, "she's that good a gym helper?"

Victoria started, "Yeah, but she's more than —"

I cut her off. "Do we really want to ruin our afternoon by talking about gym?" I walked off with Claire and Hailey, but I was too sweaty to try anything on.

7 BLACK SHEEP

It was the day of my first game with the Spikin' darn Vikings. I hacked and coughed loud enough for my mom to hear me. If she trusted me at all, I could be up in bed and home sick from school. My only decision would've been talk shows or the movie channel. Instead, Mom gave me tea and told me how powerless I was.

"Until you get your grades up, you have no say in this family on what we do, what we eat, where we go, and how we run things. All my decisions are final. You're going to school."

It was hard to take me seriously in my pajamas.

"My throat really hurts."

"Is it because you have a test today?"

Cough. "No."

"A project?"

"No!" Cough.

"Emma, I wish you'd take responsibility for yourself. Those friends are such a bad influence and they're —"

"Mom, stop."

"I bumped into Claire's mom the other day."

I nodded as she went on to tell a long, sad story of Claire and what a mess she was making of her life, but I couldn't listen. I started to sing in my head, but I couldn't keep a beat over the droning of my mother.

Before I knew it, I was listening to morning announcements and "O Canada" blaring on the PA. Somehow my five classes rushed by. I seemed caught in a time warp that was hurling me toward the volleyball court and my future as a jock.

★★★

I'd never had any background experience, like having a boyfriend to cheat on. But standing in that uniform, I felt like I was cheating on my friends, and even myself. My first game was moments away. All I had to do was open the door and enter the gym. Instead, my head found the closest toilet and I gagged up nothing but air.

The crowded gym swallowed me up as I skittered to the Spikin' Viking's bench like a crab. My head was hanging low, and I held a water bottle to cover my face. Most of the girls were bumping the ball back and forth. I sat on the bench and scanned the other team and the small crowd for anyone who might recognize me. Thankfully, no one I cared about would spend an afternoon watching middle-school sports.

A ball bounced hard in front of me and Zoe appeared. "Hey, Emma."

I faked a smile.

"So, I was thinking that you shouldn't play today."

Now, I could take that as either a nice gesture or an insult. What dots did Zoe want me to connect? "Okay," I replied.

"We all put a lot of time and effort into our game. You've only had a few practices. Plus, you don't seem that into it."

"You're right." I tapped the bench with my hand. "I'll be right here. Go, team."

"That attitude is exactly what I'm talking about. The rest of us have a relationship. We are friends and that really comes out in our —"

She needed to be cut off. "Got it."

Victoria and the other Vikings started to gather around to watch the drama.

"No, you don't."

"Talk to the coach. I'd be happy to never have to be in this gym again."

Zoe turned to the other girls. "She doesn't care about volleyball and doesn't want to be on this team."

I felt like I was being crowded. What was this? A volleyball intervention? I stood my ground by standing up. The Vikings took a step back.

Victoria piped up. "Zoe's right. We're here to win."

Some girls started shooting me dark looks and

talking angrily to others. I knew people were going to be talking about this tomorrow. "Look, I don't want to be an issue. I'm just going to sit here and you all can pretend I don't exist."

One girl called out, "'Fraid you'll break a nail?"

It was clear that reason was being left behind here. Maybe being defensive would work. "You should be 'fraid I'm gonna break your neck!" I said, moving up in her face.

Coach Marshall's voice rang out, "Hey, hey, stop that!" He made his way between me and the rest of the team. "Everyone back off, now! We have a game to play."

I slid back down on the bench.

"Come on, Vikings," he said. "I want you all to work together. That means helping out our new team member. Now, get your hands in here."

Everyone formed a circle and put their hands in the middle. *This is exactly how a zit farm can start*, I thought.

"You too, Emma," the coach said.

My hand went in, hovering above the others. I mumbled, "Go, team," before dragging myself onto the court. *Do this*, I told myself, *and it'll prove to Mom that I deserve my life back.*

The Tornadoes took the court opposite the Vikings. They looked tough. The first set started and the rest of my team tried to squeeze me out of every possible play. We dropped the set 15–25.

Standing on the back line next to the server, I was happy to be that much closer to the end of the game.

The Tornadoes sent the ball up in the air and toward me. I stepped up before anyone else and quickly gripped my hands together. I reached for the ball. I missed. It hit the ground and bounced. I felt the ball smash into my chin, ramming my head back.

The ref called, "Time!" I left the court. I collapsed on the bench, pressing an icepack against my chin.

Coach Marshall said, "Nice try, Emma. But you should have let your team know you were going for the ball. Then someone could have got it before it attacked you back. If you don't communicate, you might as well quit and take up golf. This is a team sport. Right?"

I returned to the court, the bottom of my face still deep-freeze cold. I hated my mom for forcing me to be here. I didn't belong, and I didn't want to. I should be hanging out with my friends, doing the great and sometimes stupid and useless things we like to do. The whistle interrupted a great memory of Hailey, Claire, and me persuading a high-school boy to let us into a movie for free.

The whistle blew again, this time louder and directed at me. *Well, excuse me for standing in the wrong spot.*

The Tornadoes served and our back line managed to pop it forward. A thought invaded my lack of concentration. What would Hailey do if she were stuck doing this?

Zoe, playing front and centre, set up the ball high. She must have made a mistake, because it was coming straight for me. I just wanted the game to be over. *They want tall girl*, I thought, *I'll give them tall girl.*

I raised my left hand, braced for pain, and slammed the ball over the net and into the court on the Tornadoes' side.

It took both teams by surprise. I couldn't believe it myself. I won back the serve, and my hand didn't hurt. I recoiled when the Vikings approached. What now? They reached in to high-five me and pat me on the back. The attention felt weird.

Coach Marshall yelled out at me, "Way to go!"

I ignored him. Our serve soared over my head and the Tornadoes scrambled to get it. There was too much speed on the ball, and their return volley came too close to the net. I stood with my arms up and, as they tried to get it over, I blocked it. Without thinking, I celebrated with a fist pump in the air. Then I quickly hid it in a gesture to smooth my hair.

This time the girls crowded around me, jumping up and down like monkeys.

One girl — *Courtney?* I thought — said, "Girl, you're on fire."

I shrugged. "No biggie. Just a silly game."

"What are you talking about? That gave us twenty-five."

"And . . .?" This mattered to me how?

"We won the set!"

"Then we're done?" I was so ready to take off.

Courtney smiled. "It's best of three sets. So let's win the next one."

I smiled. Win or lose, I had to get out of there.

The ref blew his whistle, forcing us back into position. I wasn't playing to win, but the Spikin' Vikings didn't seem to care. They just liked it when I used my height. My favourite part was seeing the front line of the Tornadoes back away from the net. I scared them, and at least that was fun. We took the second set, not that I cared. The coach called me a force to be reckoned with, whatever that meant.

Happily back in my clothes and out of the locker room, I listened to Zoe spout her team-captain wisdom. What I didn't understand was why I was smiling. Smashing that ball over the net felt great. As Zoe droned on, some of the other girls told me I was a good player and they were glad I was on the team.

"Hey, nice game." Oh, no. From behind me came the last voice I wanted to hear say that. It dripped with sarcasm.

I turned to see Hailey and Claire. "Hailey, this isn't what it looks like. It's not like I want to be on the team ..."

"That is exactly what I was talking about!" Zoe said, turning on me.

"Then you lied to us about not being on the team," said Hailey. "Emma, you're either with us or against us. Let's go."

The Spikin' Vikings took a step back and suddenly I was alone, caught in the middle.

I looked at Hailey and Claire. Claire wouldn't meet my eyes. "What are you guys doing here, anyway?" I asked.

"Looking for our friend."

My heart raced. How could I get out of this mess? I took a few steps toward Hailey and Claire. A peek over my shoulder revealed a bunch of angry Vikings ready to attack.

"So, that's your choice?" Zoe asked.

I whispered to Hailey, "They're not that bad."

She curled her lip angrily and said, "You playing sports is a total betrayal of our friendship. It completely trashes the image I've helped create for you."

I looked at Claire. She gave me a blank stare. I took off, out the front doors of the school into the pouring rain, and didn't stop until I got home.

8 OUT OF THE BLUE

A day later and the texts were still pouring in like there was a warehouse full of Hailey droids armed with cell phones.

Hailey: who knew you were such a jock
Claire: lol. What a jockstrap!

I shouldn't have been surprised. But that hurt.

Hailey: wait til jeremy finds out!

Trying to push the reset button on my life, I entered Mr. Marshall's class before the bell. I held out my hand with my uniform scrunched inside. "I quit."

He chugged on his coffee and sat on the edge of his desk.

"Okay."

"Good." I pushed the uniform closer to him.

"So you're going to go back to just helping the team?"

"No, I quit-quit."

"You can't quit-quit. There is an arrangement between your mom and me."

"I hate the team. I hate volleyball. I hate . . ." I stopped myself.

He smiled. "No, please. Go on."

I dropped my uniform on his desk and took off. In damage-control mode, I looked for Hailey and found her on the tarmac outside the school. I wanted to approach her, but I couldn't. I turned to my phone.

Emma: peace offering? i messed up.

I watched as Hailey picked up my text. She put the phone back in her pocket.

Emma: ok I'm sorry. Listening to mom and joining team was stupid

Nothing. The bell rang and I lined up at the back of the class. It was time to try Plan B.

Emma: i screwed up. can u help me?

Claire: I don't know what to do.

Emma: just talk to her ok?

There was no response. I watched them talk and felt locked out. But I knew Claire. She wasn't going to do anything to get Hailey as mad at her as she was at me. She wouldn't even eat if Hailey hinted that she shouldn't.

Upstairs at our lockers, they did a good job of keeping their backs to me. I went to check myself in my mirror and stopped. Hailey and Claire were starting to laugh. I stretched my neck out to see them talking to a girl named Sydney. She was the kind of girl Hailey would never have talked to. But that was before I betrayed our friendship. Hailey was replacing me.

I jumped ahead in line to get to them. "Hailey, enough! What do you want from me?" Everyone was staring at me, but I didn't care.

Hailey turned to face Claire and Sydney. At least I was talking to the side of her face, not the back of her head.

"Are you that offended?" I asked. "I didn't want to tell you about the team because I knew something like this would happen. And, yeah, they're all just using me because I'm a super-tall freak of nature, but it's better than cleaning up after them. And I can't quit because my mom won't let me." That was it. All I could do was wait for Hailey to respond.

"You're a total loser." Her voice was loud enough for the entire hallway to hear. "I don't ever want to hear you, see you, or, most of all, smell you again."

I nodded, trying my best to hold back the tears.

"Claire, help?" It was worth a shot.

Claire looked at me, then at Hailey — and then away. They both were freezing me out.

Before Hailey had entered my life, at least I had Claire. Now I had nobody. As I walked back to my spot at the back of the line, I felt more alone than I ever had in my life.

★★★

In the gym, the Vikings sat in a circle around Coach Marshall. They were all in street clothes except for the coach. He looked up at me and said, "Have a seat."

Zoe and some of the girls turned and frowned. I could feel the tension brewing, as I found a spot.

Zoe asked, "Coach, what's this meeting about?"

"I have a gift for everyone." He grabbed and held up a blue backpack. "I can't tell you all how shocked I was to see the arguing before last game. We're a team and teams don't do that." He unzipped the backpack. "Out here on the court, there's no mom or dad, no false friends or enemies, just a court and four walls occupied by people who love to play the sport. When I was your age, I played basketball. My coach reminded me that to be good you have to let go of your distractions and get into the zone. When I show up here I am fully in the zone for all of you. I put my life on hold because I want to. That's the headspace you all need if we're going to have a chance this season. After all, we're playing to have fun, but also to win. Any questions so far?"

The gym was silent. I wondered if this was a bad time to slip out.

"So, here's my gift." He flipped the backpack upside-down and a colourful rain of strips of paper and markers hit the ground.

I was confused, and I could see that mirrored in all the faces around me. Coach Marshall told us each to grab a piece of paper and a marker.

"Here's how it works," he explained. "Everyone's got stress, pressure, teen angst — whatever you want to call it. We carry it around on our shoulders into every situation. Day after day, it starts to weigh us down. I want you to write one thing that you'd like to get off your shoulders. It can be anything you want, big or small."

Zoe asked the same question on my mind. "Isn't that kind of private?"

"No names," said the coach. "Not your own or anyone else's. This won't be shared with anyone, including me. I promise not to read them."

It felt like a test or a trick that everyone was in on but me, and I was worried about writing down the wrong response. Before I knew it, I was the only person not writing. But I felt like I had so much to say that I didn't know if it would fit on the page. I thought about writing something like *the only difference between friends and enemies is that I know who my enemies are.*

Courtney asked, "Can I have more paper?"

The team broke out laughing.

Coach Marshall replied, "Use the back."

Her, "Already did," got an even bigger laugh.

In thick marker I printed out: *The people who hurt me the most are the people who swore they never would.*

It felt good to get out what I was feeling about Hailey.

Coach Marshall opened the backpack wide. "Now crumple up the paper and throw it in here."

I tossed mine at the same time as everyone else, but mine *accidentally* bounced off the coach's head. *Maybe I should go out for basketball,* I thought. *I have nothing to lose.*

Coach Marshall zipped the backpack shut and secured it on his shoulders. "Now my gift to you is that I'm going to carry your stresses on my shoulders."

"For how long?" Zoe asked.

"However long you want me to. The point is, the season's young. Let's start over this way. Because if you're not having fun, why are you here?"

It felt like his question was aimed directly at me. And the answer was even stranger. I realized that, without Hailey and Claire in my life, the only thing I had was volleyball.

Coach Marshall got to his feet. This time he did talk directly to me. "How you doing? I'm Coach Marshall. This is our team uniform. This should fit perfectly."

I took my jersey and shorts.

When the coach used a key to lower the basketball net, I wondered if he had lost it. Or if he could read my mind when I bounced the paper off his head into the backpack.

"In honour of my basketball years, we're going to play a little game called Bump. You'll go head to head with a partner in line. Your goal is to use a volleyball bump to get the ball into the net before your partner. Elimination rules, and your first shot has to start at the three-point line."

Everyone scrambled. By the time I moved, I got the last spot next to someone whose name I'd forgotten. I didn't really clue in to how the game was played until I was next to go. When it was my turn, my partner got her shot off before me but missed. I tossed my ball into the air, formed my grip, and rebounded it up and over the top of the basketball net.

Cheering erupted from the girls who were already out. I grabbed my volleyball, tossed it, set it, and watched it roll around the rim and slip into the net before my partner got hers in.

Zoe and Courtney had eliminated their partners and were coming my way fast. I darted around them and back in line to find I was up against Victoria. Zoe three-pointed her shot and Courtney was knocked out. Zoe would play Victoria or me.

I set and bumped my ball. It hit the side of my arm and spun wildly toward a wall. Luckily for me, Victoria did the same. I chased down my ball and knew I couldn't sink it from there. So I did little bumps as I walked back, like dribbling in the air.

Victoria's ball flew over my head, hit the rim, and rolled away. I let the ball bounce before bumping it up and right into the net. Victoria stormed off.

The cheering got really loud as Zoe prepped her shot. She got it off by the time I reached the three-point line. So I smacked my volleyball with my back to the net.

Everyone fell quiet. Zoe's volleyball was about to sink into the net. Coming out of the blue, my ball rammed hers off the board — and dropped into the net.

I stopped and looked at her. What now? Zoe looked at me. "Best two out of three?"

I nodded and we stepped back in line.

9 TICKLED PINK

I was surprised to get a call from Courtney and even more surprised to be asked to her house for a team get-together. I had no clue what to expect. I'd spent so long spending time with no one but Hailey and Claire that I felt like I was from another planet.

When I arrived, Courtney's mom answered the door. She walked me into the family room, where the team had taken over the entire space.

Courtney smiled at me and said, "So glad you're here." She seemed to mean it. She pointed to the volleyball game on the huge TV. "Girl serving right now is my hero, Liz Cordonier."

Who's my hero? I wondered. "Nice," I said, careful not to show how out of place I felt.

"She helped the UBC Thunderbirds get a perfect 27–0 season and was named the top female athlete in Canadian university sport. Liz also plays for Team Canada."

I nodded, a little overwhelmed by the energy in the room. I grabbed the last spot on the couch. Courtney's mom was getting us soft drinks and seemed happy to have so many people invade her nice home. The family pictures on the wall looked nice too. So were Courtney's volleyball trophies on display. *This is nice*, I thought, echoing the only word I'd said so far.

Zoe clapped her hands and said, "Okay. Let's get started. We have loads to do."

We do?

"Let's start with appreciations. I'll go first." She cleared her hair from her eyes. "Um, I'd like to thank Courtney for letting us meet here today."

The thank-yous circled the room. Victoria offered her appreciation. "I want to thank Courtney for the perfect set at the end of last game. I don't get to smash much, and it was awesome."

"It was a rainbow serve and that girl was going for the pot of gold!" Courtney exclaimed.

Huh? Everyone laughed except for me. While the team continued, I took out my phone, thumbed my way through a Hailey hate text, and googled the words *rainbow* and *volleyball*. A lingo page appeared, revealing that a rainbow was a type of serve that tries to hit the back line of the court. I was going to explore the page, but I heard my name.

Zoe was in the middle of her sentence. ". . . and she plays a mean game of Bump!"

I smiled and covered my phone. "It was fun."

The room fell silent. Looked like it was my turn. "I

wasn't supposed to be on the Vikings," I started. "Um, I guess I'd like to thank everyone for including me today."

"Okay, that's everyone!" exclaimed Courtney. "So next up is our team cheer. Last year's was good, but we can do better. Emma probably hasn't heard it unless she was at a game."

I shook my head, trying not to laugh. Team chant?

"Let's do it for her." The entire team broke into a loud, rhyming cheer. "*Viking's our name, volleyball's our game. Green and red are our colours and we bring nothing but the best game!*"

They all looked at me. I didn't know what to do, so I clapped.

"So what do you think?" Courtney asked.

It's just okay, I thought, *nothing too inspiring*. "I like it," I said. "Very, uh, cheery."

Zoe jumped in. "To come up with our new cheer, let's break into teams. We can choose the best one. Like a competition."

I ended up in a group with two girls I didn't know and one I didn't like. That one, Zoe, took charge.

"I want it to be fun and cool and all that, but also send a message," she instructed us.

The other two girls, Anita and Julie, had tons to say. They came up with, "*Let's go, get into the rhythm and flow. Come on Vikings, go-go-go!*"

Zoe scrunched up her face at that, so we started from scratch. I could hear another team in the kitchen.

It sounded like they were having fun.

Julie shared something she had scribbled down. "Got something, but no ending. Okay, here I go. *'You might be good at hockey, you might be good at baseball, but when it comes to volleyball . . .'* That's all I got."

"It doesn't rhyme," I said.

All three girls looked at me like I had majorly offended Julie. "Okay, no rhyme," I said. "How about, *'But when it comes to volleyball, you better watch your back.'*" Based on their reaction the answer was a giant nope.

"Come on," Zoe said, "we don't want to be undone."

Not having spent face-to-face time with Zoe before, I now had enough to start a profile. *She's got an A-type personality and she doesn't like to be a) outdone and b) wrong.* She reminded me of my mom. No wonder we weren't getting along.

We took a short break to brainstorm on our own. Brainstorming together wasn't working. I got up to stretch and made my way to the window. Courtney tapped me on my shoulder.

"Everything okay?" she asked.

"Yeah," I said.

"So I have to ask. What's the story with you and Hailey?"

"We used to be friends."

"Used to be?"

"Well, the story, it's kind of long."

"I asked because some rumours are spreading."

I could guess where they were spreading from.

"And the volleyball part?" Courtney added.

"My mom forced me to volunteer. Then the coach cornered me into playing."

"'Cause you're tall."

My back stiffened. *Was this an ambush?*

"Oh, I didn't mean it as a bad thing," Courtney said when she saw my reaction. "Trust me, we're all jealous."

I didn't know how to take the mention of my height as a compliment.

Courtney explained, "You've got a — no joke intended — head up on us when it comes to getting into a sports high school and maybe even a university scholarship."

I had never thought about my height that way.

"Last get-together," Courtney laughed, "Zoe made us do these stupid upside-down stretches to get blood flowing up to our brains. Like that would make us grow! And as much as I would like to be Liz Cordonier, she is over six feet tall and I never will be."

"You don't know that for sure."

"Have you seen my parents?"

I smiled. It ran like a chant through my head: *T is for tall, T is for terrific, T is for terrible. Go team!*

Courtney's group called her back, so I checked in with mine. Zoe looked up at me like I was the enemy.

I turned to Julie and Anita. "Anything good enough yet?"

Zoe said, "If you don't have any ideas, then don't interrupt."

I couldn't just take that. I decided to switch my *T* to a *V* and stumbled through a cheer. *"V is for victory, V is for Vikings. We've got game, bumps, sets, and spiking. So bring it on, 'cause we're the Spikin' Vikings."*

There was a silence, and then Anita and Julie started laughing and clapping. They liked my cheer so much that they practically forced Zoe to support it. I was surprised when Zoe admitted that they hadn't come up with anything as good.

We presented the cheer when the team was all back together. We acted out the bumps, sets, and spikes.

"Who came up with that?" asked Courtney. "And why didn't we have a cheer this great last year?"

I secretly enjoyed it when Zoe had to admit the cheer was mine. "Julie and Anita came up with the actions," I said. *Take that, Zoe.*

The cheer competition went to a blind vote. My cheer won.

10 BLACK AND BLUE

Bump and set before hitting. I rehearsed in my head like I was about to go on stage in front of hundreds of people. The stage was actually just the volleyball court, and there were only about twenty-five people crowded into the gym. I was thankful that I couldn't see anyone I knew in that twenty-five people. Still, I had butterflies.

First period that morning I smirked when Coach Marshall wore the blue backpack to math class. All period, he had deflected questions from other students about what was inside. Now he was pacing back and forth on the sidelines with it on. I knew the crowd was wondering what was with the backpack. I could hear the whispers about it.

The ref blew his whistle, and I followed the girls onto the court. They raised their hands, began to skip and form a circle. I walked my way into the circle.

Zoe took the lead. "This is our game. Those Lions are awfully cute and cuddly, but they're going down. Let's cage them and send them back to the zoo!"

The girls howled with laughter, breaking off into their positions. I took the back-left corner.

The Lions started the game off with a bang, getting two quick points before we could win serve. So much for Zoe's inspiring pep talk. When we finally won serve, it didn't last. The Lions scored four more points and then it was my turn to serve. *You can do it*, I told myself. I lifted the ball into the air. I was just about to smack it when I heard the whistle.

The ref pointed to the ground.

"What did I do?" I asked.

Anita turned to tell me, "You stepped over the line."

"And you lost us the serve," Zoe added.

Anita called for the ball. I bounced it to her and she rolled it under the net to the Lions.

"It's a stupid rule," I said. There was no way that the Lions hadn't picked up that I was the rookie. Praying for the ball not to come my way, but knowing that it would, I stood with my knees bent and my right foot forward.

The Lions' server pounded the ball into our zone, over Courtney and in front of me. Courtney was quick to step back and bump the ball. It went in with too much heat and bounced out of play. The next serve came right at me. I smacked my wrists together, pointed my thumbs down, and rebounded the ball high. Victoria, her hands in front of her face, set up the ball to Zoe — surprise. Zoe smashed it over the net. The rest of the Vikings met in the middle of our zone to hug and high-five while I shuffled to the centre-back corner, following the clockwise rotation.

We were on a roll.

We were winning by one when Julie served it high and deep. The Lions managed to return it. I stuck in my spot, unsure if I was supposed to go in and help at the net or stay back. I watched the play, my knees bent and hands glued together, ready for anything. The ball found its way to me, coming off a smash from their front line. I jumped forward, pressing my arms in its path. The volleyball thundered off me and right over the net, where the Lions easily smashed it for a point.

Zoe was quick to attack me again. "You're supposed to bump and set it!"

Before I could bark back, Courtney said, "It was coming in too fast and low. At least she got to it."

Zoe wiped sweat from her face with her black wristbands. "Emma, we can't get ahead with you on the team!"

The ref blew his whistle and called out to Coach Marshall. "Do we need a timeout, Coach?"

Courtney pointed to her foot and called out, "Shoelace!"

The ref gave her a moment to tie it.

My only supporter on the team pulled me down with her to say, "Ignore Zoe. Emma, there's gym class volleyball and then there's league volleyball."

I nodded, totally in the dark.

She formed a loop with one end of the shoelace. "What I mean is that, to some people, this is their whole life. So just try your best and don't take anything too personally."

"Oh, I get it. Thanks. Anything else?"

"Yeah. Don't step out of position until the ball's been served. And if you're at the net and the other team is serving, turn and follow the ball so you can see the set." Courtney tightened her shoelace and stood up. "You need to know when to go for it, but sometimes the best move is to just get out of the way."

I nodded, trying to memorize her advice. "Thank you, Courtney," I said, and I meant it.

The next Lions serve arced deep into our corner. Julie dove for it, her hands still somehow locked together even when she hit the ground. She managed to bump the ball up at me. Ready for the set, I extended my hands in front of my face, cushioning the ball before sending it high to the front line. With Zoe and Victoria hogging centre and left, I gave it to Courtney, who slammed it into the Lions' court.

After joining the team for a quick celebration huddle, I moved one spot over in the rotation to the back and left position. Courtney tossed the ball up and smacked it over the net. The Lions bumped, set, and returned the ball. We did the same. The volleyball finally curved in my direction. I braced for a bump but Zoe stepped back to take my shot. It went over the net, barely, and she got the point.

Our next serve soared over the net. The Lions got a handle on the ball quickly and set it up perfectly for their front attack line. Zoe and Victoria formed a wall, their arms up. They jumped as the ball came their way, and I saw my chance. Stepping forward, I leaped into the air as the ball trickled over their fingertips. Not knowing whether to bump or set, I just slammed the ball as hard as I could. Gravity pulled me back to earth and I watched the ball hit the Lions' court for another point.

When we met for a quick moment in a circle, no one was more stunned than me that I had pulled that off.

Breaking out, Coach Marshall announced, "We have the lead!"

Maybe it was my point that changed our momentum, but in any case we won that tight set. After a much-needed water break, I headed across the court to switch sides for set two. What I saw stopped me dead in my tracks.

Hailey stood on the sidelines, giggling.

I lowered my head. Why was she here? She turned, and I noticed that it wasn't Claire she was giggling to.

Jeremy stood next to her.

Had they been there the whole stupid game? The idea of them together felt like a kick to my stomach. *Just relax,* I told myself. Even though I felt like Jeremy was cheating on me, he barely knew I was alive.

Then Hailey put her arm around Jeremy and pulled him close.

A tide of jealousy ran through me. I didn't know whether to cry, run, or curl up in a ball. I took a deep breath. It was now clear that Hailey had officially declared war.

A ball landed at my feet and jolted me back to reality. The play had gone on without my noticing.

Zoe snipped, "Hello. Earth to moron!"

I blurted, "It was going out," without looking at her or the ball. We lost serve, and I looked for reasons to care. I knew I needed to take my anger out on the volleyball or I was going to blow up in a fiery display of fury.

The Lions delivered the ball. When the set came my way, I set up for a smash repeat that would knock my first one off the spike-ometer. I drew my hand back like a hammer and slammed my fist at the ball. But it didn't feel right. Just air. And then a face full of pain. The volleyball had passed by my hand to smack me in the face.

I dropped, my dead weight crashing to the court and onto my ankle. I rolled over, trying to grab at both my ankle and my face.

Lying on the court, I closed my eyes.

After a moment, the coach appeared next to me. "You okay?"

I tested my ankle. The pain had definitely dulled a bit.

"I don't think it's broken," he said, touching it gently.
"It hurts."

I knew that if I stayed down, I could go home. If I stretched it out, I could probably miss school for a day or two. I could get off the team. Then I pictured Hailey and Zoe cheering, and I slowly got to my feet.

A small applause filled the gym.

Coach Marshall shooed the rest of the Vikings away and held his arm out for me. "Can you put pressure on that ankle?"

"I'm okay."

"You don't look it. Come on, let me take you to the bench."

"No. I'm okay."

"Are you dizzy? It's not just your ankle. You got tattooed."

"Huh?"

"You've got volleyball seams on your face."

I turned to see Hailey getting a good laugh from my misfortune. Tattooed or not, I was going to keep playing. Coach Marshall finally backed off and I took my position in front of the net, tenderly touching my nose. *Get back in the game*, I muttered to myself as I saw Anita set the ball to me.

I tracked the ball, but it seemed to change course, bending past me. Hand up, I swatted and missed it, nearly toppling over.

"Okay, I've seen enough!" called out Coach Marshall.

He grabbed my arm and guided me off the court.

As good as it felt to sit with a pack of ice on my face, I hated that Hailey stuck around just to see us — me — lose.

11 ULTRAVIOLET LIGHT

The loud beat of the dance music thumping from huge speakers pulsated off my sweaty skin. I stood alone against the gym wall, hiding out in the dark.

Hailey kept close enough to let me know she was watching me. Zoe was chatting up the Spikin' Vikings, making sure they all knew how lame I was.

I surveyed the dimly lit world in front of me. The DJ bobbed up and down on stage, one headphone held to his ear, in his own world. Most people were in huddles, except a few boys who were too awkward to know that dancing by yourself, arms flapping, was the definition of grotesque. I searched the depths of my jean pockets for change so I could buy a drink, but came up with just shreds of lint.

Since being released from Hailey's comet and being without a BFF — or any friends at all — people off my radar were prowling around me. I turned my eyes down. Staring back at me was the out-of-bounds line from the volleyball court. The sight of it made me feel woozy. In need of fresh air, I made my move to the gym doors. I was stopped by Zoe.

She got right down to business. "Don't show up for the tournament," she screamed over the music.

"Not your place to say that," I yelled back.

"I want to win. Why don't you leave the team?"

I was impressed that she wanted me out that badly. "You're worse than Hailey!" I mumbled.

"What?"

"Nothing."

"Theft and betrayal. What do you gain from telling everyone our secrets?"

"What are you talking about?"

"I'm going to prove it." She spun away.

"Nice to see you too," I yelled at her retreating back. *She's just jealous*, I told myself, remembering what Courtney said. Besides, it was the coach's call to keep me on the team or not. I sidled along the edge of the gym to the doors. It was a roundabout way, but it would keep me out of the limelight. It didn't work.

"There you are!"

I stopped and turned. "Hey, Courtney."

The music was still pretty loud, even away from the speakers. She leaned in to hear me better. "How are you feeling after yesterday's game?"

"I went to bed early and rode the spinning that was my room like I was in the middle of a tidal wave."

She smiled gently. "You got hit hard."

I ran my finger along my cheek. I could still trace the shallow imprint from the seam of the ball.

"Some call it getting tattooed," Courtney said. "I prefer *getting a six-pack*."

The song ended, overlapping with the start of another. "Why?" I asked.

"It's the same sensation as having downed a six-pack of beer. Not that I've tried beer before."

The way she laughed made me suspect a cover-up.

"Emma, we've all experienced it before. Hurts for about two days."

I thought about the backpack. I wasn't the only one on the team with secrets and problems. Courtney was talking about my external pain, but she couldn't sense that I was feeling like garbage inside. What I needed was a hug. Not that I would never ask for one.

"And your ankle?" Courtney asked.

"It's okay. Really, I'll get over the pain. But I am happy to be on the team." Where did that come from? Even stranger, I realized it was the truth.

"I'm glad, too. It's kind of a switch for you, isn't it."

"Yeah, my old life kind of took a nose dive. I guess without this team I'd have nothing." That wasn't entirely true. I had become almost a brain. Without all the distractions and drama of being Hailey's friend, and no one to text to, I had been forced to pay attention in class. My latest math quiz and science test scores were both in the high Bs.

"I'm glad to hear that. So you don't talk to Hailey at all?"

"Are you kidding me? She hates me. Hates me even more because I play volleyball. But, whatever."

Courtney laughed. "She's an intense girl."

"Yeah. Controlling, too."

"Then you're better off without her."

I nodded and smiled. Maybe Courtney did understand me.

"I've had friendships turn bad before. It doesn't seem like it now, but you'll get over it."

"I hope so, because right now Hailey's a twenty-four/seven pain."

"Take that energy and put it into volleyball. Oh, volleyball. That reminds me. I totally forgot to tell you!"

I took a hopeful step toward her, my mind racing. *Did something horrible happen to Hailey? Did she finally get in trouble? Who was pressing charges?*

"Coach Marshall's backpack is missing." Courtney spoke behind her hand.

"Really? Did someone steal it?"

"Don't know. No one knows anything yet."

"Coach Marshall is extremely upset," Courtney went on. "Especially because of what's inside."

A weird cramp shot through my body. "All our secrets!" My secret!

"Luckily he was smart enough to make sure our names weren't on anything. But whoever did it could put two and two together. It wouldn't be hard to figure out that it's us. I feel sick."

Who would want to hurt the team? Hurt me? It had to be Hailey. No fingerprint analysis or bogus alibi needed. This had Hailey written all over it. *Case closed*, I thought.

"Courtney, what if it gets out? Oh my god." Another realization hit me with a thud. "Zoe thinks I did it?"

Courtney nodded. She pointed her finger at me in the shape of gun and pulled the trigger. "I didn't want to be the one to tell you. I'm sorry."

12 GREY MATTER

Stomach on bed, legs bent in the middle and up against the wall, I scratched an itch with the balding eraser end of my pencil. In front of me lurked my math homework. Without anybody to call, chat, or text with, it was just me and it. "Your life is officially boring," it mocked me. The thrilling world of rectangular prisms replaced girl talk, gossip, and other reasons to not do homework.

Until I heard the footsteps, the only noise in the house was the faint sound of some TV show playing downstairs. Footsteps turned into a pitter-patter, then the sound of a triple knock on the door and the turn of the handle.

It started with a pointed finger. "You're always on that thing."

"Mom —"

"No, no excuses. You're up late because of that phone." She was still at the door, her head tilted like she was too weary to keep it up anymore. "And when you don't get sleep it makes you snippy and you can't focus in class. And that just causes stress for you and everyone else."

I finally clued in that all she could see was the glow of my phone. The crumpled bed sheets blocked my math textbook and workbook. I kept quiet and let her go on.

"Now, I'm not saying you don't need a phone. These days, it's a safety thing. Better to have it than not. But your dad and I pay for your phone, so we should have some say as to when you use it."

"But —"

"No, I've given this a lot of thought. This is not negotiable. A friend of mine put her daughter's phone on seasonal standby. She can still make emergency calls, but that's it."

I knew that she was talking about Claire. I was there when her mom did that. It had happened two years ago, and had lasted about a month.

It was time to cut Mom loose. And I could make her feel a touch bad along the way. I held up my phone so she could see the screen.

When she saw the calculator app, her face relaxed and the pointy finger dropped down to her side.

I evened out the bedsheets to reveal my math homework. Mom's head returned to its upright position.

"Sorry," she said. "It's just that I —"

"It's okay, Mom. Can you sign my math quiz?"

"That's a good mark," she said, looking at the quiz and taking my pencil.

I nodded.

Once she had signed the quiz, she left. It was how she came in, but in reverse. She stepped out of my bedroom, closed the door, and released the handle. The pitter-patter dulled to distant footsteps, until all I could hear was the faint sound of the TV.

★★★

At school, the news broke quickly. Coach Marshall was on the hunt for his backpack and would stop at nothing to find it. People who weren't even on the team were tuned into the drama. The usual suspects were thrown into the guilty pile, including a random bunch of weirdos and a flock of girls with anger issues who tended to go off like dynamite. And also a boy named Tristan, who previously had in-school suspensions and a very rare out-of-school suspension for theft of school property. According to my now-limited gossip channels, Hailey wasn't even on the list. I thought about reporting her, but who would believe me? Hailey's most notable crimes to date were incomplete homework, late projects or assignments, distracting boys in class, and the application of too much eyeliner. She never got caught at anything more serious because she got her friends to do her dirty work.

When we arrived at the gym for practice, Coach Marshall was quiet. It was the kind of quiet I experienced from my mom after my Grandmother Sherry died. I had heard that some of the girls' parents had complained and piqued the interest of Principal Hastings. Coach Marshall must be in hot water.

"Hello, everyone," he said. "I don't have to tell you what the deal is. You've all heard."

His voice was distant and his head was down. Was he in danger of getting fired? Did I need to step forward, even though I had no evidence? All I had were some suspicions strung together about an ex-friend who'd like to see the newest member of the team get deep-fried.

Coach Marshall looked up at us. "Look, I thought the backpack was a good idea at the time. And it did help us work together, play together . . . I saw that." He scratched at some stubble on his chin. "I know a lot of you didn't like the idea of sharing your personal stresses and worries in life, so I apologize for that."

I raised my hand halfway and waited for him to nod.

"It was strange at first," I said. "But I think it was a good idea."

"Thank you, Emma," Coach Marshall replied. "I guess, in theory, it was."

Zoe was clearly peeved that I spoke before her. She broke in, "We were all talking — well, most of us — and we want to help you find it."

"I appreciate that. I do." If Coach Marshall saw the way Zoe stared accusingly at me, he didn't show it.

I thought, *Here comes the witch-hunt.*

Coach Marshall looked tired. "If one of you is upset and did this out of spite or something, please just return the backpack . . . or keep the backpack and return the pieces of paper. Those thoughts are yours, not mine, and I want to return them to you. There will be no questions asked, no blame laid." He inhaled deeply. "Practice is cancelled this afternoon. Thank you for coming. That's all."

★★★

Back in class, Courtney plopped herself next to me. "I think I have figured it out."

"What?" I asked.

"You've got two bullies. Both Zoe and Hailey have it in for you."

I said, "They do?"

"Yeah, it's pretty obvious, Emma. Hailey's acting like you don't exist and Zoe clearly wishes you didn't."

I stared at her. How did she see that? Had I become that see-through?

"You see," Courtney explained, "Zoe knows she can't be a pro volleyball player and Hailey can't be a supermodel because neither of them are tall enough. You are."

I nodded. "So, Master Yoda, what do I do?"

"Oh, you don't have to do anything. It's what they have to do."

I lifted my eyebrows at her.

"The only thing that will fix this is if they get on each other's shoulders."

I laughed hard. It felt good to laugh with someone again.

"Want to join me for some extra volleyball practice after —" Courtney was cut off, by a loud, horrible thud.

My head whipped around. It took a moment for me, and a little longer for everyone else, to see that it was Claire. She was on the ground. I felt like time had stopped. Then I shoved my chair out and rushed to her. I beat the teacher there and slid onto the floor, placing my hands under her head to support it.

Suddenly time sped up and chaos broke out in the classroom. The French teacher, Madame Newman, madly punched numbers into the phone to reach the office. Most of the boys, old enough to machine gun people in their online games, were too immature to deal with reality. They stood there and snickered.

"Claire," I said. Nothing. Her eyes were shut like she was sleeping. There was nothing peaceful about the way her legs were splayed, knees bent in an awkward position. I called her name again. This time her eyes fluttered open and then closed just as quickly.

"Hey!"

I looked up to see Hailey barrelling toward me from the door. She was returning from the washroom for, I think, the third time.

She yelled, "Get away from her immediately."

"I'm her friend, too," I said quietly.

"Claire hates you. She wants nothing to do with you."

I gently placed Claire's head on the floor.

"What did you do to her?" Hailey asked angrily.

"Nothing."

"I know you've been looking to get back at me," Hailey hissed. "But this is how you do it?"

I bit back with, "Shut up, Hailey! You know she fainted because you got her to stop eating lunch!"

The onlookers reacted with an "Oohh."

We both turned as there was a soft whimper from the floor. Claire's eyes opened and she tried to sit up.

"No, just stay where you are," Hailey said in a soft voice. She dropped to her knees beside Claire.

Claire looked at Hailey and then at me. She was clearly confused. It was Hailey who looked like Claire's BFF.

I got to my feet and disappeared behind the curtain of people surrounding the scene.

Madame Newman and another teacher rushed past me as I dragged myself back to my desk.

"Okay, everybody, go back to your seats," Madame Newman ordered. The other teacher, trained in first aid, got Claire to a chair. "Anyone know what happened?"

I raised my hand and spoke at the same time. "I think she didn't eat her lunch."

Hailey was on her feet, supporting Claire. "Madame Newman, she has the flu."

"Claire, is that true?" asked the teacher.

Claire nodded.

Lies, I screamed in my head!

Claire patted the back of her head. "My head hurts."

Once Claire, Hailey at her side, had followed the teacher down to the office, the classroom returned to normal.

Courtney appeared beside my desk again. "Are you okay?" she asked.

"Yeah. I need to get a drink." I left the class and rushed down the hall. I went right past the fountain and kept going.

I hated Hailey. I hated even more that I seemed to be losing every battle against her. If she could play dirty, why couldn't I? Why wasn't *I* sending *her* mean-spirited texts twenty-four/seven?

Then I thought of Claire. My real loss in the fight with Hailey was not getting to be with Claire. I had met her first and have known her the longest. I suddenly knew that the only way to get to Hailey would be by winning Claire over to my side. But how could I break Hailey's control over Claire when I had been happily in the same spot for so long?

13 WHITE FLAG

Rumours about Claire floated around the school like bubbles. All air, no substance. In class, I tried to focus on a reading response for a book I had actually read, the first in a long time. I felt my phone sending me a *look-at-me* buzz. I tried to ignore it, thinking it was probably another of Hailey's hate letters. But I saw that she was at her desk, hands not buried in her lap. I snuck a peek. A Facebook notification appeared with the words, *you have to check this out.* I moved to the pencil sharpener on the counter, my back to the classroom, and swiped through the notification to a fan page called *Pretty or Not.*

A cold feeling ran down my back.

I thumbed down and saw a picture of Claire. With her hair done and a ton of makeup, she was so dolled-up I hardly recognized her. Then there was me. I was horrified to see the photo Hailey snapped in the hallway when we were still friends. I wondered if she would be stupid enough to have her name on this. I could report her right away. The page read *hosted by anonymous*. Finally hearing the whining of the little motor at my stuck pencil, I pulled my fingers back before the sharpener could do its work on those too.

Back at my seat, I took out a book and used it to block my phone. A grey box on the screen caught my eye: *Cast your comment and thanks for voting*! Below that I found the familiar words, *Like, Comment*, and *Share*. This was a competition I didn't want to be involved in.

The page refreshed and a post appeared below the photos.

gladiator99: hey you ugly pork bellies, do the world a favour and drop a few pounds.

The vicious comment stung. Actually, it hurt. I looked up to get a bearing on the teacher and then returned to "my book."

AlexK: the tall one is definitely not. looks aren't everything but in your case they are nothing!

I shut off my phone, disgusted that Hailey would set me up like this. How could she do this to me? Needing out, I threw my name on the washroom sign-out board. I took off down the hallway and into the girls' washroom. I lodged myself in a stall, the door locked. My first instinct was to punch a hole through the door. Instead, I growled, my voice bubbling with anger.

Another buzz from my phone caught me off guard. Then another. As much as I didn't want to look, it was like a car accident. I had to.

iJulie: There are more important things in life . . . Focus on people who wake up hungry or who don't have freedom.
CarleyM: Have some self-worth and don't put yourself online like this, girls. If you were my daughters I'd make sure you were never online again.

I dangled my phone over the toilet. I imagined it clogging the pipes and sending flooded water all over the floor. A caretaker would dig it out and would know it was mine. I put the phone back in my pocket.

Footsteps echoed in the tiled washroom and I slinked back onto the seat. The water ran for a moment. I tried to get an ID through a sliver separating the stall door from the wall. She had her back to me, but I saw her face when she looked into the mirror.

Hailey looked right back through the mirror. She said, softly and slowly, "Surprise."

I lurched back, almost dropping into the bowl butt-first. "What do you want?"

"You might think it's to win, prove a point, or squash you until you're a nobody, just like before we were friends."

I held my breath.

She went on, "Or to keep Claire away from you. But it's not."

Somehow, I found my voice. "Posting our pictures is the cruellest thing you've done."

"Hey, I cut you a break. The mean thing would have been to actually declare war. I could have the entire school against you in no time."

"What do you want?" I repeated.

She didn't respond and for a moment I wondered if she was still there. I put out a feeler, making sure what I said was not a question that would leave me open for a jab. "You're here to give me a second chance."

"The last chance," she corrected me.

Claire must have talked to her, begged her.

"Last chance at what?" I asked.

"Friendship."

Huh! Trapped in the stall, I wished I had one of those lawyers like on TV. *Judge, my client has been nothing but nice to this so-called friend turned bully. Your Honour, it was the defendant who threw their friendship overboard into shark-infested waters. And now her intentions are, frankly, confusing. Will she throw my client a line? Let the record show that we will not drop the charges and we will not settle. My client's looking for a guilty plea, plus one million dollars for emotional damages . . .*

The damage had been done. I couldn't forgive and forget everything she put me through. *That's it,* I thought, *the only response that makes sense.*

I heard the door open. Hailey said to the girl, "Closed. Find another one." "This offer is only good until I walk out the washroom door."

A big part of me wanted nothing more than to have a do-over. I wanted to roll back time to before Mr. Marshall met with my mother. I wanted to return to a time when everything I did and thought revolved around planet Hailey. I missed her crass jokes, her mean, laugh-my-butt-off comments about other people. I missed knowing that her friendship meant I was worth something.

Looking through the crack, I softly said, "Okay, Hailey, you win."

There was no response.

Slowly unlocking the stall door, I pushed it open to find that Hailey had vanished. Was I losing it? Was she even there to begin with?

★★★

The tacky waitress in the cowboy hat returned with more tortilla chips and asked, "How y'all doing so far?"

I wanted tell her to take her fake accent and refill my Diet Coke but stopped myself. It wasn't her fault that my mood was spiralling into a bottomless pit. My phone rumbled in my pocket, so I snuck a peek at that instead.

HollywoodHaze: The one on the right looks like a gerbil has been gnawing on her face.

That was me on the right. I cringed.

My mom took a sip of her margarita. "Ninety percent on your math test, Emma. We are very proud."

I nodded, my chip half wedged in the salsa and about to snap under its weight.

My dad said, "It's not the marks, but the effort that we appreciate."

Snap!

"I know it's wrong to offer bribes," my mom added. "But a couple more grades like those and a shopping trip will be in order."

I sent in a rescue chip.

"That sound good?" my mom prompted.

I smiled. Not for the shopping, but for the success of the salsa rescue mission.

Cowboy boots clattered, signalling the arrival of dinner. My food sizzled and spat like it was angry. "Portions are humongous," said the waitress. "So don't be 'fraid to ask for a daw-gee bag." She took off.

"And the volleyball?" my dad asked. "How's that going?"

"Okay," I said through my last bit of salsa-covered chip.

"Can we come watch?"

"It's pretty much just students who come to the games." I took a tester bite off my iron plate. "Have you thought at all about a sports high school?" he pressed.

"Why would they want me? I don't really consider myself an athlete, Dad."

"Well, have a look at their website sometime. You're on a team, so that's good. And it's only a short bus ride."

My phone burped. I looked down, pretending to actually consider what my dad was saying.

pkscarlet: Mom and dad should consider boarding school. Lock you up and throw away the key!

"Think about it," my dad suggested. "Maybe ask a guidance counsellor."

"We don't have one."

"Then a teacher. Course selection starts soon and it can't hurt to apply. But if it makes you uncomfortable, then don't."

I had another bite of food and read another message on the *Pretty or Not* site.

VandaWalle: It's not you, it's your generation. I remember feeling the same way and I never had Internet. Reach out to someone else — friends and family — this is not the place. Give yourself a break — it's not uncommon to feel this way. If you were mine, I'd make you feel like the beautiful human being you are. What you really need is a hug. Stay away all you cyber freaks.

Finally a nice person.

SadlerH: You're both as ugly as it gets!

I pushed my plate away from me and shut off my phone, vowing to never turn it on again.

14 RED-HANDED

Slurping on my water bottle did little to quench my thirst after an intense volleyball practice. Coach Marshall, still reeling over the missing backpack, took it out on us in the form of laps. During a scrimmage game, I used my height advantage at every turn to send the message to Zoe that I was not backing down. *As sad and pathetic as it is*, I reminded myself, *this team is all you have right now.*

Zoe waved Coach Marshall over. "Coach, any word on the missing backpack?"

"I really don't have anything to tell you at this time." He looked sorry.

"We've been talking about it and we're all worried."

He looked annoyed at Zoe's persistence. "Yes, I am too. At least no names were on anything."

"But whoever took it, they'll know."

"It's an inside job!" Victoria said.

"If it makes any of you feel better," sighed Coach Marshall, "I got chewed out about it. Let's just say I'm not in the principal's good books anymore."

Zoe looked at me as she said, "I wish the person would have the guts to just admit it."

"Or return the backpack anonymously. Anyway," the coach said, "go get changed and have a good afternoon, everyone."

He turned to go, but Zoe stopped him. "Don't you want to talk about the tournament tomorrow?" "Tournament?" I said. But no one responded.

"Oh, yeah, that," said Coach Marshall. "There will be a lot of good teams playing, so get a good night's sleep."

Not exactly motivating, I thought. The moment I stepped into the locker room, the conversation switched back to the missing backpack.

Zoe barked at me, "Emma, just 'fess up, already!"

"I didn't do anything!" I yelled back.

"We all know you took it!"

"You need to back off right now."

"Or what?"

"Or else!"

Zoe paused. I don't think anyone on her precious team had ever stood up to her before. She said slowly, every word a threat, "We don't want traitors on our team."

I turned to the rest of the team and asked, "Is this the way a team captain is supposed to act?"

No one answered. I hoped that Courtney might stand up for me, but I couldn't blame her. What good would it do her to get on Zoe's bad side?

I turned back to Zoe. "Okay, captain, tell me right now, what proof do you have? We're all here. We're all listening. Share your proof."

"We never had any trouble on this team before you joined it," Zoe said. "And you don't even want to be on the team. So everyone thinks you took it."

"That doesn't make me guilty." It was a good point, not that anyone cared. "Proof! What proof do you have? You have nothing or you'd have already taken it to the principal."

Zoe stepped in close to me. I didn't know if she was going to punch, yell, or spit. When she did none of those things, I stepped back, got changed, and left.

★★★

The next day, I looked up from my math problem sheet to find a surprise guest in the classroom. Principal Morrison stood at the doorway. Her fingers were so tightly intertwined, her knuckles were white.

Coach Marshall — now Mr. Marshall, math teacher — asked us to put down our pencils. He explained, "Principal Morrison is here because we received an anonymous tip about the missing backpack." Courtney and I exchanged curious looks. The class exploded in talk and my stomach sank. I was having one of those *I-have-a-bad-feeling-about-this* moments.

My eyes darted to Zoe. A small, uneven fault line cracked across her face.

Principal Morrison clapped her hands and shut down the talk. "I've had to do this only once before in my career as a school principal," she said. "We're having a locker search."

I didn't move, blink, or breathe. I ordered myself to calm down, thinking that, since I didn't take the backpack, I had nothing to worry about.

Zoe was quick with a question. "Why check everyone?"

"I don't want to single out anyone. Our information could be wrong. As well, you all need to know that we can't check your lockers for something like the backpack without your permission." She held out a piece of paper. "Sign next to your name if you're okay with us doing a quick search. If you have any issue with this, then don't sign."

The paper started to slither its way around the room. I wasn't sure if I was going to sign. A quick scan of the page when it hit my desk showed me that all the girls on the team had signed it. Except for a few boys and one kind of radical girl, everyone had signed. This was my chance to prove my innocence. Jotting my signature, I joined the line snaking to the hallway where everyone was asked to stand on the wall across from his or her locker.

"To be completely fair, we are searching the lockers of all the grade-eight classes," the principal announced.

"If your locker is clear, go back to class and continue what you were doing."

The search started. With each locker, I was one step closer to clearing my name. I wondered how the Vikings would react when Zoe was proved wrong. Maybe they would elect me captain after Zoe was forced to be a bench warmer.

In military style, Coach Marshall checked the list, and called out a name. The student stepped forward to open the locker and then stepped back so the principal could rifle through it. When the all-clear was given, the locker was closed, and the student locked it and returned to class.

Halfway through and still no backpack. *How can Zoe be so sure of herself?* I wondered. Then a sickening realization hit me. What if it was Zoe who took the backpack? Or Hailey? Either way, someone could have set up everything leading to this moment and planted the backpack in my locker. Zoe would win by getting me suspended and out of the tournament the next day. Hailey would win by humiliating me in front of the whole school, and losing me any friends I might have started to make.

Hailey opened her locker. No backpack. Courtney was next. Same thing. There was just Zoe, another boy, Claire, and then me. Sweat started to form on my forehead and I discreetly wiped it away. I might be innocent, but it looked like I was going down for this crime.

Zoe, smiling, opened her locker and said, "Tada!"

Nothing. Her locker was so neatly organized it was like she was expecting visitors. She looked at me as she walked back toward the classroom, one eyebrow slightly above the other.

If you act guilty, you might as well be, I told myself, looking away from Zoe's retreating back. *When your turn comes, just step forward, unlock, quick look, lock it, and you're back at the wall, a free woman.*

The next locker took some force to yank open. Then a flood of papers, binders, pencil cases, books, and even a metre stick cascaded out, forming a giant heap on the floor of the hallway.

The remaining suspects watched as the principal picked up a library book and announced that she needed to speak to the owner of the locker after class. The guy had signed the locker search sheet. Maybe he wanted to be found. But still no backpack.

I spotted Hailey leaving the class to take a drink of water — or at least to pretend to. Her lips never had and never would touch that fountain. But she had to be there to witness my humiliation.

Claire stepped forward. She spun her lock dial three times past zero, then left to 27, then right to 8, and left to 13. I knew the combination as well as I knew my own. And Hailey knew that Claire had mine memorized too. Claire stepped back from her locker, revealing her red backpack. Hanging beside it was a blue backpack. Coach Marshall's backpack.

So it was Hailey. I couldn't wait to celebrate my freedom from Zoe's pointy finger and sly comments, but my focus was on Hailey. She wore a complete look of shock. She was behind this, I just knew it. But how did the backpack end up in Claire's locker instead of mine?

Coach Marshall looked sadly at Claire. "Why?"

Claire shrugged.

"You have nothing to say?" asked Principal Morrison.

"It was something to do," Claire replied. She looked at me for a very brief moment. "I thought it'd be fun."

15 PINK SLIP

I just wanted to forget about everything and get to the game. *Do what coach said*, I told myself, *and leave the stress behind*. I was in and out of my locker in seconds and was the first one changed and in the gym.

The net was up and so were signs pushing drinks and snacks for spectators. I never thought I'd be happy to be in the gym, warming up. In the middle of a full leg stretch, with my head almost down to my feet, I spotted the rest of the Vikings enter the gym. I was greeted by a welcoming committee of Zoe and Victoria.

Zoe asked, "What are you doing here?"

I stood so I would tower over her. I was beginning to see my height could be an advantage, and not just on the court. Even though we were on the court. Out of the corner of my eye, I saw Courtney on her way.

Courtney jumped right in and said, "This is not the time —"

I cut her off. "Thanks, Courtney, but I've got this." I took a step toward Zoe. "I proved my innocence and you were proven wrong. So unless there's an apology coming in the next few seconds, get out of my face." It felt great to let her have it.

"Actually, I do have something important to say."

Ready to focus on getting ready for the game, I asked, "What more could you possibly have to say, captain?"

Zoe looked at Victoria for a moment and they both smiled. "It's because I'm captain that I can get you off the team. Or at least keep you from playing." My feet were cemented to the ground, but in my mind I was out the door, out the school, down the street, and half-way home.

Victoria asked Zoe, "What is she still doing here?"

I bolted out the gym doors, trying my hardest to stop my tear ducts from bursting. I wasn't going to cry in school. Out the front doors of the school, I headed across the parking lot and out to somewhere where I could sob, weep, bawl, and wail. Then I heard my name.

"Emma. Stop!" Coach Marshall caught up to me.

"Please leave me alone."

"You don't have to leave."

I turned away. I didn't want him to see me cry. "Yes, I do. No one wants me anywhere, especially not on the Vikings."

"Then just take this."

He handed me a brown envelope. "What is it?"

"You can open it," he said.

I pulled a folded letter from inside.

"It's a glowing report of your hours spent with the Vikings. Look, the team kinda fell apart. The missing backpack didn't help. But the team was better because of you. Thank you."

I nodded. Both of us stood in the chilly air with nothing but an awkward silence between us.

"Emma, one more thing," Coach Marshall broke the silence. "You're brave and tough. When you're older, you're going to make a difference in this world. So be your own person. And, if you don't mind me saying, you're better without Hailey."

"I appreciate the honesty, Coach." *But*, I thought, *I'm not better without Claire.* "Hey, if we don't have that, what do we have? So I'll be honest with you. You shouldn't drink so much coffee."

"I appreciate that. And I am trying to cut down."

"To what? A bucket a day?"

He laughed and we walked back to the school. We stepped in the doors just in time to hear the school's PA blaring from above. The voice was the office secretary ordering me to report to the office.

Coach Marshall held his hands out. "Don't look at me."

I walked into the office and was asked to have a seat. I had just gotten comfortable when I was asked to go into Principal Morrison's office. I was shocked to see Zoe and Hailey already there.

"Go ahead, Emma," the principal said, "Have a seat."

All I could think was that Zoe must have been upset to be missing the first game of the tournament. And that Hailey would rather be anywhere but at school

Principal Morrison started, "I have to say that I'm quite upset to have you girls in my office. Let's just say that while I was looking into the missing backpack, I started to have serious concerns about bullying. I shouldn't have to remind any of you that our school has zero tolerance for that kind of behaviour."

She turned to me. "Emma, I want you to know that I'm taking the allegations of bullying seriously. Let's start with Zoe."

Zoe glared at me. She thought I had ratted her out. I couldn't even look at Hailey.

"For the record," Principal Morrison said, "I have not spoken to Emma before now. She did not come forward."

Thank you, I said silently.

"So, Zoe, there have been reports of bullying on the girl's volleyball team. Do you have anything that you want to tell us about?"

Both Zoe and Hailey were different in the principal's office. Under her thumb, they were much less threatening.

Zoe took a long time without saying anything. Then, "I guess I never really thought that what I was doing was bullying. I just wanted everyone on the team to want and deserve to be there."

Principal Morrison looked at a list on her desk. "Yelling at Emma, excluding her, accusing her, trying to get her off the team. All that is bullying, Zoe, especially when, as captain, you are in a position of trust and authority."

Zoe looked like she might cry, but she was dry-eyed when she said, "There are no excuses for the things I said to Emma. And I did it in front of the team, which is how you probably found out. It was wrong."

"Okay," said the principal. "We appreciate your honesty. Emma, would you like to respond?"

The spotlight was on me, but I wasn't short for words. "Zoe, I know I came on your team late and I brought a lot of issues with me. And I understand why you wouldn't like me. You know, accusing me of stealing the backpack didn't hurt as much as you not giving me a chance."

Zoe nodded.

"Zoe," the principal reminded her, "now would be a great chance for you to do what we talked about."

Zoe perked up. "Emma, I'm sorry for being mean to you."

I didn't know what to say. Thank you? No biggie?

Principal Morrison excused Zoe and she slithered out.

The principal closed one file and opened another.

One bully down, I thought, *another one to go.* If Hailey could throw out a quick apology, I'd be happy. Everyone could go home for the night.

"Unfortunately the situation with Hailey is quite a bit more serious."

There went my dreams of getting out of there.

Principal Morrison scanned a page in the file. "Hailey, you initiated a cyberbullying attack against Emma. You anonymously posted a picture of her and got people to respond if they thought she was pretty or not. Not only did most of the student body see this, but so did strangers out there in the cyberworld." She added a small note to the file.

"Let's deal with the security issue first. Both of you, please check and reset your privacy settings. Only people you know and trust should be able to see your social network page."

I nodded. Hailey didn't budge.

"Hailey, the apology we need from you isn't as simple as Zoe's. We're dealing with school rules and even laws. Now, about the backpack. Why did you steal it?"

"I didn't," said Hailey. She even managed to look surprised.

"You didn't steal it with plans to put it in Emma's locker and have her take the blame?"

Hailey shook her head. Her hair was tied back, her makeup perfect, and she didn't look guilty or scared at all.

Principal Morrison leaned forward. "Your mother has been notified and she's on her way to pick you up. This is very serious. You will be getting a suspension for two days. It will go on your record. There will be additional punishment if we find that you've lied. My advice to you is to tell the truth."

Hailey stared off somewhere very distant, probably wishing she was at the mall.

"Did you steal the backpack?"

She shook her head.

Principal Morrison stood up and left her office. For a brief moment it was just Hailey and me. I wouldn't have been surprised if she full-out attacked me. Then Principal Morrison entered the office with a surprise witness.

16 SILVER LINING

"Jeremy?" This was the last place and time I thought I'd see him.

He took the seat Zoe had left. His eyes were down, refusing to make contact with mine or Hailey's.

"Jeremy," the principal started, "did you steal the backpack?"

His voice was so low I could barely hear it. "Yes, I stole it."

"But why?" I asked.

"Because Hailey asked me to."

Hailey jumped out of her chair. "Come on, Jeremy!" She turned to the principal. "He's lying."

Jeremy spoke softly through Hailey's denials. "She told me that Coach Marshall took her backpack and that she needed it back because her phone was in there."

"That's not true," Hailey protested.

"I didn't know it wasn't her backpack until the word spread that the volleyball team really wanted it back." Jeremy looked up for the first time. "Will this be on my record?"

Hailey answered with, "You're such a jerk."

Jeremy kept his eyes on the principal. "I'm planning on going to the sports high school and —"

"You did the right thing when you found out you were lied to," Principal Morrison offered. "While it was an innocent, but reckless, mistake, it will require consequences. But I don't think your bright future will be stalled by this."

Jeremy nodded, returning his gaze to the ground until he and I were excused.

I stood in the hallway, not knowing what to do. In the distance I could hear the sounds of the volleyball game. In the office behind me was the person I thought would save my life, and then who almost destroyed it.

It wasn't long before Hailey was on the other side of the principal's door. She stared at me through the small window and I looked back, feeling sorry for her. It felt like an hour that we looked at each other, but must have been less than a minute. Finally, a voice broke in.

"Emma, I haven't seen you in forever."

I turned to see Hailey's mother. She didn't stop to talk on her way to meet Principal Morrison about her delinquent daughter.

I made my way to the gym. Zoe appeared through the doors as some game-play noise escaped. "Why aren't you playing?" I asked her.

"Our first game's done. We won."

"Cool."

"Emma, I meant it when I said I was sorry. And I realize that what the team needs is you on it. Do you think you might want to have your spot back?"

I thought about it for a moment. It was a nice gesture and it made Zoe's apology that much more real. But I wasn't sure who I was or what I wanted anymore. Was I really a sports jock, or was I just letting people use me because of my height? If there was a voice inside my head, directing me, it wasn't clear. "Thanks, Zoe, but I think I'm going to pass."

She was stunned. Strangely, so was I.

"Thanks, but no thanks," I repeated.

Zoe nodded and said, "See you in class."

Before I went to get my stuff from the locker room, there was someone I needed to speak to. I stepped into the gym and headed for Coach Marshall. "Coach," I said, getting him to notice me.

When he turned to me, I started in on him, "I don't appreciate you going behind my back to the principal. I can handle my own problems."

"Emma," he said, ignoring my frown. "I'll admit to pushing you to give volleyball a try. You think it's because of your height. But if I were coaching cross-country or soccer, I would've done the same thing. You might not want to hear this or believe it, but you're an athlete."

"But I don't know what else you think I've done," he went on. "Whatever is happening with the principal beyond looking for the backpack, I have no idea. Zero."

"Honestly?" I asked.

"Honestly," he nodded. "Look, I have a game to coach in five minutes. I wish you were going to play in it, but you have to go where you feel you belong. Please drop your uniform off in the locker room on your way out."

Feeling stunned, I nodded. Trudging across the court, I took in the crowd and the Spikin' Vikings running a cheer, the cheer that I helped come up with.

"V is for victory, V is for Vikings. We've got game, bumps, sets, and spiking. So bring it on 'cause we're the Spikin' Vikings."

Inside the locker room I was alone. It was over.

"Hi."

Startled by the voice, I almost hit the ceiling. It was Claire, sitting on a bench and chewing gum. "You know," she said, "It doesn't smell that bad in here."

I wanted to laugh — or cry. We had been friends forever. Why didn't I know what to say to her now? Maybe start with a question. "Claire, why was the backpack in your locker and not mine? Or Hailey's?"

"I couldn't let Hailey's plan to set you up work. But I didn't want Hailey to get in trouble. If Jeremy hadn't gone to the principal, stupid me would have taken the blame for Hailey and that backpack forever."

I sat. "Why?"

"This is going to sound ridiculous. She's a friend."

"And you're an amazing friend to do that. She doesn't deserve you."

Claire smiled. "You're so right. That girl has some serious issues. She needs help."

I nodded.

"So, on the posting," Claire went on, "you were voted prettier than me."

"And you're telling me because . . ."

"You should be happy."

"Claire, I don't know why you're here or what you want, but you're stunningly beautiful. In fact, we both are. And hearing that I won some twisted game that Hailey made us play doesn't make me happy."

"I should go." Claire stood up and moved toward the door.

"It was nice to see you, Claire. I'm really glad you're feeling better."

She stopped. "I'm sorry that I forgot how to be a good friend. I'll understand if you hate me forever. Especially since you've made a real friend on the team. Who do you think went to the principal about the bullying?"

"Claire —"

She cut me off. "Can I say one last thing?"

"Sure."

"You're lucky to find something you're good at. You're an awesome volleyball player. I think you're throwing away something special if you just quit."

She left and I was alone in the locker room. I waited for the voice in my head, because there were two choices . . . two doors. One led to the hallway and home, and the other led back into the gym.

★★★

Maybe I was wrong. Maybe I was making a decision I'd regret. But I couldn't predict the future. I just knew that, halfway home, the *what-ifs* would start and never stop.

Coach Marshall was pacing back and forth. I caught him off guard.

"Coach?"

He turned away from the game for just a second. "Hey, Sherlock, you have to take off the uniform to get it in the locker room."

"I want back on the team."

Zoe saw us and called a timeout. "What's wrong?"

Coach Marshall said, "Emma wants back on the team, but I don't know."

"Let her play," Zoe said.

The coach pointed at the bench and said to me, "Warm up that bench and I'll think about playing you."

"Yes, sir."

"It's Sir Coach."

"Yes, Sir Coach."

He smiled and I sat on the bench. Courtney waved at me from the court. I needed to thank her for going

to the principal about Zoe later. I could thank someone else right away. I turned on my phone and waited
for the clutter of texts and notifications to stop before
texting.

Emma: thanks for being a good friend.

Claire: What took you so long?

Emma: interested in getting a friend back?

Claire: Yeah!

"Emma," Coach Marshall called out, "I'm subbing
you in."

"That was fast."

"Got a problem with that?"

"No."

He looked at me.

"No, Sir Coach," I corrected myself.

I tucked my phone under the bench and stepped
onto the court, high-fiving Julie on the way to her spot,
front row and centre.

The Tomahawks had serve, and I wished I had a moment to figure out everything that had happened that
day. But the volleyball soared over my head. I turned
with it as Courtney managed to control its spin by
bumping it high toward the net. "Ball's up!" she called.

Zoe stepped back, nearly touching the net. She
was half a step from being out of bounds. "Mine!" she
called out. With her hands pressed out in front of her,
she set up the ball. I knew it was up to me to make
the play.

A perfect set by Zoe sent the ball along the net to me. "I got it!" I positioned my arms forward and stepped toward the net. Moving faster, I swung my arms back, my palms straight up behind me. At the net, my arms came forward and I leaped off the court. At the top of my arc above the net, I wound my right arm back. I swung through the ball just before gravity dragged me back down. I held my balance long enough to see two Tomahawks players dive for and miss my spike.

Zoe helped me back onto my feet and said, "That was incredible!" She dragged me toward the others for a quick but loud celebration.

I joined in the cheer. *"V is for victory, V is for Vikings! We've got game, bumps, sets, and spiking. So bring it on 'cause we're the Spikin' Vikings!"*

Pumped and back in position, I scanned the crowd and spotted Jeremy. He gave a small wave.

I'd been afraid of changing. But suddenly I realized that life without Hailey as my BFF would be just fine. Not a bad ending for what had been the worst, and definitely the best, day of school ever.

ACKNOWLEDGEMENTS

A big thank you to Carrie Gleason for believing in this story and supporting it from the initial pitch. Thanks to my editor Kat Motatsune, who has such an incredible eye for detail. You uncovered elements in the story and helped to weave themes together. Thank you to Nicole Habib, project manager, for putting the finishing touches and seeing my book into print. Thank you to teacher, colleague, and friend Matthew Sherlock, who helped develop the character of the coach. And thank you to my family for their continued support. My wife inspired this book. She played sports all throughout high school and university and it opened doors to her future.

According to the Women's Sport Foundation website: "By age 14, girls are dropping out of sports at twice the rate of boys. When they walk away from sport, they walk away from their potential."

Sports are important for individuals to be social, active, problem solve, develop teamwork and have fun. We must continue to find ways to support and encourage girls to get involved and realize the benefits of group sports and the doors they open.